TOGETHER AT LAST!

A great embarrassment fell upon him as he entered the grounds of the Macdonald place, and when he stood before the plate-glass doors waiting for an answer to his ring he would have turned and fled if he had not promised to come.

It was perhaps not an accident that Ruth let him in herself and took him to a big quiet library with wide-open windows overlooking the lawn. To his great amazement, he could feel at once at ease with her and talk to her just as he had done in her letters and his own.

Somehow it was like having a lifetime dream suddenly fulfilled to be sitting this way in pleasant converse with her, watching the lights and shadows of expression flit across her sensitive face, and knowing that the light in her eyes was for him. . . .

Tyndale House books by Grace Livingston Hill.
Check with your area bookstore for these best-sellers.

COLLECTOR'S CHOICE
SERIES

1 The Christmas Bride
2 In Tune with Wedding Bells
3 Partners
4 The Strange Proposal

LIVING BOOKS ®
1 Where Two Ways Met
2 Bright Arrows
3 A Girl To Come Home To
4 Amorelle
5 Kerry
6 All Through the Night
7 The Best Man
8 Ariel Custer
9 The Girl of the Woods
10 Crimson Roses
11 More Than Conqueror
12 Head of the House
14 Stranger within the Gates
15 Marigold
16 Rainbow Cottage
17 Maris
18 Brentwood
19 Daphne Deane
20 The Substitute Guest
21 The War Romance of the
   Salvation Army
22 Rose Galbraith
23 Time of the Singing of Birds
24 By Way of the Silverthorns
25 Sunrise
26 The Seventh Hour
27 April Gold
28 White Orchids
29 Homing
30 Matched Pearls

32 Coming Through the Rye
33 Happiness Hill
34 The Patch of Blue
36 Patricia
37 Silver Wings
38 Spice Box
39 The Search
40 The Tryst
60 Miranda
61 Mystery Flowers
63 The Man of the Desert
64 Miss Lavinia's Call
77 The Ransom
78 Found Treasure
79 The Big Blue Soldier
80 The Challengers
81 Duskin
82 The White Flower
83 Marcia Schuyler
84 Cloudy Jewel
85 Crimson Mountain
86 The Mystery of Mary
87 Out of the Storm
88 Phoebe Deane
89 Re-Creations
90 Sound of the Trumpet
91 A Voice in the Wilderness
92 The Honeymoon House
93 Katharine's Yesterday

CLASSICS SERIES
1 Crimson Roses
2 The Enchanted Barn
3 Happiness Hill
4 Patricia
5 Silver Wings

THE SEARCH

LIVING BOOKS ®
Tyndale House Publishers, Inc.
Wheaton, Illinois

This Tyndale House book
by Grace Livingston Hill
contains the complete text
of the original hardcover edition.
NOT ONE WORD
HAS BEEN OMITTED.

Living Books is a registered trademark of Tyndale
House Publishers, Inc.

Printing History
J. B. Lippincott edition published 1919
Tyndale House edition/1992

Library of Congress Catalog Card Number 92-80580
ISBN 0-8423-5831-5
Printed in the United States of America

99   98   97   96   95   94   93   92
8   7   6   5   4   3   2   1

I

TWO young men in officers' uniforms entered the smoker of a suburban train, and after the usual formalities of matches and cigarettes settled back to enjoy their ride out to Bryne Haven.

"What d'ye think of that girl I introduced you to the other night, Harry? Isn't she a pippin?" asked the second lieutenant taking a luxurious puff at his cigarette.

"I should say, Bobbie, she's some girl! Where d'ye pick her up? I certainly owe you one for a good time."

"Don't speak of it, Harry. Come on with me and try it again. I'm going to see her friend tonight and can get her over the 'phone any time. She's just nuts about you. What do you say? Shall I call her up?"

"Well, hardly to-night, Bob," said the first lieutenant thoughtfully, "she's a ripping fine girl and all that, of course, but the fact is, Bob, I've decided to marry Ruth Macdonald and I haven't much time left before I go over. I think I'll have to get things fixed up between us to-night, you see. Perhaps—later—. But no. I guess that wouldn't do. Ruth's folks are rather fussy about such

1

things. It might get out. No, Bob, I'll have to forego the pleasures you offer me this time."

The second lieutenant sat up and whistled:

"You've decided to marry Ruth Macdonald!" he ejaculated, staring. "But has Ruth Macdonald decided to marry you?"

"I hardly think there'll be any trouble on that score when I get ready to propose," smiled the first lieutenant complacently, as he lolled back in his seat. "You seem surprised," he added.

"Well, rather!" said the other officer dryly, still staring.

"What's there so surprising about that?" The first lieutenant was enjoying the sensation he was creating. He knew that the second lieutenant had always been "sweet" on Ruth Macdonald.

"Well, you know, Harry, you're pretty rotten!" said the second lieutenant uneasily, a flush beginning to rise in his face. "I didn't think you'd have the nerve. She's a mighty fine girl, you know. She's—*unusual!*"

"Exactly. Didn't you suppose I would want a fine girl when I marry?"

"I don't believe you're really going to do it!" burst forth the second lieutenant. "In fact, I don't believe I'll *let* you do it if you try!"

"You couldn't stop me, Bob!" with an amiable sneer. "One word from you, young man, and I'd put your captain wise about where you were the last time you overstayed your leave and got away with it. You know I've got a pull with your captain. It never pays for the pot to call the kettle black."

The second lieutenant sat back sullenly with a deep red streaking his cheeks.

"You're no angel yourself, Bob, see?" went on the first lieutenant lying back in his seat in satisfied triumph, "and I'm going to marry Ruth Macdonald next week and get a ten days' leave! Put that in your pipe and smoke it!"

There ensued a long and pregnant silence. One glance at the second lieutenant showed that he was most effectually silenced.

The front door of the car slammed open and shut, and a tall slim officer with touches of silver about the edges of his dark hair, and a look of command in his keen eyes came crisply down the aisle. The two young lieutenants sat up with a jerk, and an undertone of oaths, and prepared to salute as he passed them. The captain gave them a quick, searching glance as he saluted and went on to the next car.

The two jerked out salutes and settled back uneasily.

"That man gives me a pain!" said Harry Wainwright preparing to soothe his ruffled spirits by a fresh cigarette.

"He thinks he's so doggone good himself that he has to pry into other people's business and get them in wrong. It beats me how he ever got to be a captain—a prim old fossil like him!"

"It might puzzle some people to know how you got your commission, Harry. You're no fossil, of course, but you're no angel, either, and there are some things in your career that aren't exactly laid down in military manuals."

"Oh, my uncle Henry looked after my commission. It was a cinch! He thinks the sun rises and sets in me, and he had no idea how he perjured himself when he put me through. Why, I've got some of the biggest men in the country for my backers, and wouldn't they lie awake at night if they knew! Oh Boy! I thought I'd croak when I read some of those recommendations, they fairly gushed with praise. You'd have died laughing, Bob, if you had read them. They had such adjectives as 'estimable, moral, active, efficient,' and one went so far as to say that I was equally distinguished in college in scholarship and athletics! Some stretch of imagination, eh, what?"

The two laughed loudly over this.

"And the best of it is," continued the first lieutenant, "the poor boob believed it was all true!"

"But your college records, Harry, how could they get around those? Or didn't they look you up?"

"Oh, mother fixed that all up. She sent the college a good fat check to establish a new scholarship or something."

"Lucky dog!" sighed his friend. "Now I'm just the other way. I never try to put a thing over but I get caught, and nobody ever tried to cover up my tracks for me when I got gay!"

"You worry too much, Bobby, and you never take a chance. Now I—"

The front door of the car opened and shut with a slam, and a tall young fellow with a finely cut face and wearing workman's clothes entered. He gave one quick glance down the car as though he was searching for someone, and came on down the aisle. The sight of him stopped the boast on young Wainwright's tongue, and an angry flush grew, and rolled up from the top of his immaculate olive-drab collar to his close, military hair-cut.

Slowly, deliberately, John Cameron walked down the aisle of the car looking keenly from side to side, scanning each face alertly, until his eyes lighted on the two young officers. At Bob Wetherill he merely glanced knowingly, but he fixed his eyes on young Wainwright with a steady, amused, contemptuous gaze as he came toward him; a gaze so noticeable that it could not fail to arrest the attention of any who were looking; and he finished the affront with a lingering turn of his head as he passed by, and a slight accentuation of the amusement as he finally lifted his gaze and passed on out of the rear door of the car. Those who were sitting in the seats near the door might have heard the words: "And they *killed* such men as Lincoln!" muttered laughingly as the door slammed shut behind him.

Lieutenant Wainwright uttered a low oath of imprecation and flung his half spent cigarette on the floor angrily:

"Did you see that, Bob?" he complained furiously, "If I don't get that fellow!"

"I certainly did! Are you going to stand for that? What's eating him, anyway? Has he got it in for you again? But *he* isn't a very easy fellow to get, you know. He has the reputation——"

"Oh, I know! Yes, I guess anyhow *I know!*"

"Oh, I see! Licked you, too, once, did he?" laughed Wetherill, "what had you been up to?"

"Oh, having some fun with his girl! At least I suppose she must have been his girl the way he carried on about it. He said he didn't know her, but of course that was all bluff. Then, too, I called his father a name he didn't like and he lit into me again. Good night! I thought that was the end of little Harry! I was sick for a week after he got through with me. He certainly is some brute. Of course, I didn't realize what I was up against at first or I'd have got the upper hand right away. I could have, you know! I've been trained! But I didn't want to hurt the fellow and get into the papers. You see, the circumstances were peculiar just then——"

"I see! You'd just applied for Officer's Training Camp?"

"Exactly, and you know you never can tell what rumor a person like that can start. He's keen enough to see the advantage, of course, and follow it up. Oh, he's got one coming to him all right!"

"Yes, he's keen all right. That's the trouble. It's hard to get him."

"Well, just wait. I've got him now. If I don't make him bite the dust! Ye gods! When I think of the way he looks at me every time he sees me I could skin him alive!"

"I fancy he'd be rather slippery to skin. I wouldn't like to try it, Harry!"

"Well, but wait till you see where I've got him! He's in the draft. He goes next week. And they're sending all those men to our camp! He'll be a private, of course, and he'll have to *salute me!* Won't that gall him?"

"He won't do it! I know him, and *he won't do it!*"

"I'll take care that he does it all right! I'll put myself in his way and *make* him do it. And if he refuses I'll report him and get him in the guard house. See? I can, you know. Then I guess he'll smile out of the other side of his mouth!"

"He won't likely be in your company."

"That doesn't make any difference. I can get him into trouble if he isn't, but I'll try to work it that he is if I can. I've got 'pull,' you know, and I know how to 'work' my superiors!" he swaggered.

"That isn't very good policy," advised the other. "I've heard of men picking off officers they didn't like when it came to battle."

"I'll take good care that he's in front of me on all such occasions!"

A sudden nudge from his companion made him look up, and there looking sharply down at him, was the returning captain, and behind him walked John Cameron still with that amused smile on his face. It was plain that they had both heard his boast. His face crimsoned and he jerked out a tardy salute, as the two passed on leaving him muttering imprecations under his breath.

When the front door slammed behind the two Wainwright spoke in a low shaken growl:

"Now what in thunder is that Captain La Rue going on to Bryne Haven for? I thought, of course, he got off at Spring Heights. That's where his mother lives. I'll bet he is going up to see Ruth Macdonald! You know they're related. If he is, that knocks my plans all into a cocked hat. I'd have to sit at attention all the evening, and I couldn't propose with that cad around!"

"Better put it off then and come with me," soothed his friend. "Athalie Britt will help you forget your troubles all right, and there's plenty of time. You'll get another leave soon."

"How the dickens did John Cameron come to be on speaking terms with Captain La Rue, I'd like to know?" mused Wainwright, paying no heed to his friend.

"H'm! That does complicate matters for you some, doesn't it? Captain La Rue is down at your camp, isn't he? Why, I suppose Cameron knew him up at college, perhaps. Cap used to come up from the university every week last winter to lecture at college."

Wainwright muttered a chain of choice expletives known only to men of his kind.

"Forget it!" encouraged his friend slapping him vigorously on the shoulder as the train drew into Bryne Haven. "Come off that grouch and get busy! You're on leave, man! If you can't visit one woman there's plenty more, and time enough to get married, too, before you go to France. Marriage is only an incident, anyway. Why make such a fuss about it?"

By the fitful glare of the station lights they could see that Cameron was walking with the captain just ahead of them in the attitude of familiar converse. The sight did not put Wainwright into a better humor.

At the great gate of the Macdonald estate Cameron

and La Rue parted. They could hear the last words of their conversation as La Rue swung into the wide driveway and Cameron started on up the street:

"I'll attend to it the first thing in the morning, Cameron, and I'm glad you spoke to me about it! I don't see any reason why it shouldn't go through! I shall be personally gratified if we can make the arrangement. Good-night and good luck to you!"

The two young officers halted at a discreet distance until John Cameron had turned off to the right and walked away into the darkness. The captain's quick step could be heard crunching along the gravel drive to the Macdonald house.

"Well, I guess that about settles me for the night, Bobbie!" sighed Wainwright. "Come on, let's pass the time away somehow. I'll stop at the drug store to 'phone and make a date with Ruth for to-morrow morning. Wonder where I can get a car to take her out? No, I don't want to go in her car because she always wants to run it herself. When you're proposing to a woman you don't want her to be absorbed in running a car. See?"

"I don't know. I haven't so much experience in that line as you have, Harry, but I should think it might be inconvenient," laughed the other.

They went back to the station. A few minutes later Wainwright emerged from the telephone booth in the drug store with a lugubrious expression.

"Doggone my luck! She's promised to go to church with that smug cousin of hers, and she's busy all the rest of the day. But she's promised to give me next Saturday if I can get off!" His face brightened with the thought.

"I guess I can make it. If I can't do anything else I'll tell 'em I'm going to be married, and then I can make her rush things through, perhaps. Girls are game for that sort of thing just now; it's in the air, these war marriages.

By George, I'm not sure but that's the best way to work it after all. She's the kind of girl that would do almost anything to help you out of a fix that way, and I'll just tell her I had to say that to get off and that I'll be court-martialed if they find out it wasn't so. How about it?"

"I don't know, Harry. It's all right, off course, if you can get away with it, but Ruth's a pretty bright girl and has a will of her own, you know. But now, come on. It's getting late. What do you say if we get up a party and run down to Atlantic City over Sunday, now that you're free? I know those two girls would be tickled to death to go, especially Athalie. She's a Westerner, you know, and has never seen the ocean."

"All right, come on, only you must promise there won't be any scrapes that will get me into the papers and blow back to Bryne Haven. You know there's a lot of Bryne Haven people go to Atlantic City this time of year and I'm not going to have any stories started. *I'm going to marry Ruth Macdonald!*"

"All right. Come on."

2

RUTH Macdonald drew up her little electric runabout sharply at the crossing, as the station gates suddenly clanged down in her way, and sat back with a look of annoyance on her face.

Michael of the crossing was so overcareful sometimes that it became trying. She was sure there was plenty of time to cross before the down train. She glanced at her tiny wrist watch and frowned. Why, it was fully five minutes before the train was due! What could Michael mean, standing there with his flag so importantly and that determined look upon his face?

She glanced down the platform and was surprised to find a crowd. There must be a special expected. What was it? A convention of some sort? Or a picnic? It was late in the season for picnics, and not quite soon enough for a college football game. Who were they, anyway? She looked them over and was astonished to find people of every class, the workers, the wealthy, the plain every-day men, women and children, all with a waiting attitude and a strange seriousness upon them. As she looked closer she saw tears on some faces and handkerchiefs everywhere in evidence. Had some one died? Was this a funeral train they were awaiting? Strange she had not heard!

Then the band suddenly burst out upon her with the familiar wail:

> *There's a long, long trail awinding,*
> *Into the land of our dreams,—*

and behind came the muffled tramping of feet not accustomed to marching together.

Ruth suddenly sat up very straight and began to watch, an unfamiliar awe upon her. This must be the first draft men just going away! Of course! Why had she not thought of it at once. She had read about their going and heard people mention it the last week, but it had not entered much into her thoughts. She had not realized that it would be a ceremony of public interest like this. She had no friends whom it would touch. The young men of her circle had all taken warning in plenty of time and found themselves a commission somewhere, two of them having settled up matters but a few days before. She had thought of these draft men, when she had thought of them at all, only when she saw mention of them in the newspapers, and then as a lot of workingmen or farmers' boys who were reluctant to leave their homes and had to be forced into patriotism in this way. It had not occurred to her that there were many honorable young men who would take this way of putting themselves at the disposal of their country in her time of need, without attempting to feather a nice little nest for themselves. Now she watched them seriously and found to her astonishment that she knew many of them. There were three college fellows in the front ranks whom she had met. She had danced with them and been taken out to supper by them, and had a calling acquaintance with their sisters. The sister of one stood on the sidewalk now in the common crowd, quite near to the runabout, and seemed to have forgotten that anybody was by. Her face was drenched with tears and her lips were quivering. Behind her was a gray-haired woman with a skewey blouse and a faded dark blue serge skirt too long for the prevailing fashion. The tears were trickling down her cheeks also; and an old man with a crutch, and a little round-eyed girl, seemed to belong to the party. The old man's lips were set and he was looking at the boys with his heart in his eyes.

Ruth shrank back not to intrude upon such open sorrow, and glanced at the line again as they straggled down the road to the platform; fifty serious, grave-eyed young men with determined mien and sorrow in the very droop of their shoulders. One could see how they hated all this publicity and display, this tense moment of farewell in the eyes of the town; and yet how tender they felt toward those dear ones who had gathered thus to do them honor as they went away to do their part in the great world-struggle for liberty.

As she looked closer the girl saw they were not mature men as at first glance they had seemed, but most of them mere boys. There was the boy that mowed the Macdonald lawn, and the yellow-haired grocery boy. There was the gas man and the nice young plumber who fixed the leak in the water pipes the other day, and the clerk from the post office, and the cashier from the bank! What made them look so old at first sight? Why, it was as if sorrow and responsibility had suddenly been put upon them like a garment that morning for a uniform, and they walked in the shadow of the great sadness that had come upon the world. She understood that perhaps even up to the very day before, they had most of them been merry, careless boys; but now they were men, made so in a night by the horrible *sin* that had brought about this thing called War.

For the first time since the war began Ruth Macdonald had a vision of what the war meant. She had been knitting, of course, with all the rest; she had spent long mornings at the Red Cross rooms—she was on her way there this very minute when Michael and the procession had interrupted her course—she had made miles of surgical dressings and picked tons of oakum. She had bade her men friends cheery good-byes when they went to Officers' Training Camps, and with the other girls welcomed and admired their uniforms when they came home on short furloughs, one by one winning his stripes and commission. They were all men whom she had known in society. They had wealth and position and found it easy to get into the kind of thing that pleased them in the army or navy. The danger they were facing seemed hardly a negligible quantity. It was the fashion to look on it that way. Ruth had never thought about it before. She had even been severe in her judgment of a few mothers who worried about their sons and wanted to get them exempt in some way. But these stern loyal mothers who stood in close ranks with heavy lines of sacrifice upon their faces, tears on their cheeks, love and self-abnegation in their eyes, gave her a new view of the world. These were the ones who would be in actual poverty, some of them, without their boys, and whose lives would be empty indeed when they went forth. Ruth Macdonald had never before realized the suffering this war was causing individuals until she saw the faces of those women with their sons and brothers and lovers; until she saw the faces of the brave boys, for the moment all the rollicking lightness gone, and only the pain of parting and the mists of the unknown future in their eyes.

It came to the girl with a sudden pang that she was left out of all this. That really it made little difference to her whether America was in the war or not. Her life would go on just the same—a pleasant monotony of bustle and amusement. There would be the same round of social affairs and regular engagements, spiced with the excitement of war work and occasional visiting uniforms. There was no one going forth from their home to fight whose going would put the light of life out for her and cause her to feel sad, beyond the ordinary superficial sadness for the absence of one's playmates.

She liked them all, her friends, and shrank from having them in danger; although it was splendid to have them doing something real at last. In truth until this moment the danger had seemed so remote; the casualty list of which people spoke with bated breath so much a thing of vast unknown numbers, that it had scarcely come within her realization as yet. But now she suddenly read the truth in the suffering eyes of these people who were met to say good-bye, perhaps a last good-bye, to those who were dearer than life to them. How would she, Ruth Macdonald, feel, if one of those boys were her brother or lover? It was inconceivably dreadful.

The band blared on, and the familiar words insisted themselves upon her unwilling mind:

There's a long, long night of waiting!

A sob at her right made her start and then turn away quickly from the sight of a mother's grief as she clung to a frail daughter for support, sobbing with utter abandon, while the daughter kept begging her to "be calm for Tom's sake."

It was all horrible! Why had she gotten into this situation? Aunt Rhoda would blame her for it. Aunt Rhoda would say it was too conspicuous, right there in the front ranks! She put her hand on the starter and glanced out, hoping to be able to back out and get away, but the road behind was blocked several deep with cars, and the crowd had closed in upon her and about her on every side. Retreat was impossible. However, she noticed with relief that the matter of being conspicuous need not trouble her. Nobody was looking her way. All eyes were turned in one direction, toward that straggling, determined line that wound up from the Borough Hall, past the Post Office and Bank to the station where the Home Guards stood uniformed, in open silent ranks doing honor to the boys who were going to fight for them.

Ruth's eyes went reluctantly back to the marching line again. Somehow it struck her that they would not have seemed so forlorn if they had worn new trig uniforms, instead of rusty varied civilian clothes. They seemed like an ill-prepared sacrifice passing in review. Then suddenly her gaze was riveted upon a single figure, the last man in the procession, marching alone, with uplifted head and a look of self-abnegation on his strong young face. All at once something sharp seemed to slash through her soul and hold her with a long quiver of pain and she sat looking straight ahead staring with a kind of wild frenzy at John Cameron walking alone at the end of the line.

She remembered him in her youngest school days, the imp of the grammar school, with a twinkle in his eye and an irrepressible grin on his handsome face. Nothing had ever daunted him and no punishment had ever stopped his mischief. He never studied his lessons, yet he always seemed to know enough to carry him through, and would sometimes burst out with astonishing knowledge where others failed. But there was always that joke on his lips and that wide delightful grin that made him the worshipped-afar of all the little girls. He had dropped a rose on her desk once as he lounged late and laughing to his seat after recess, apparently unaware that his teacher was calling him to order. She could feel the thrill of her little childish heart now as she realized that he had given her the rose to her. The next term she was sent to a private school and saw no more of him save an occasional glimpse in passing him on the street, but she never had forgotten him; and now and then she had heard little scraps of news about him. He was working his way through college. He was on the football team and the baseball team. She knew vaguely that his father had died and their money was gone, but beyond that she had no knowledge of him. They had drifted apart. He was not of her world, and gossip about him seldom came her way. He had long ago ceased to look at her when they happened to pass on the street. He doubtless had forgotten her, or thought she had forgotten him. Or, it might even be that he did not wish to presume upon an acquaintance begun when she was too young to have a choice of whom should be her friends. But the memory of that rose had never quite faded from her heart even though she had been but seven, and always she had looked after him when she chanced to see him on the street with a kind of admiration and wonder. Now suddenly she saw him in another light. The laugh was gone from his lips and the twinkle from his eyes. He looked as he had looked the day he fought Chuck Woodcock for tying a string across the sidewalk and tripping up the little girls on the way to school. It came to her like a revelation that he was going forth now in just such a way to fight the world-foe. In a way he was going to fight for her. To make the world a safe place for girls such as she! All the terrible stories of Belgium flashed across her mind, and she was lifted on a great wave of gratitude to this boy friend of her babyhood for going out to defend her!

All the rest of the straggling line of draft men were going out for the same purpose perhaps, but it did not occur to her that they were anything to her until she saw John Cameron. All those friends of her own world who were training for officers, they, too, were going to fight in the same way to defend the world, but she had not thought of it in that way before. It took a sight of John Cameron's high bearing and serious face to bring the knowledge to her mind.

She thought no longer of trying to get away. She seemed held to the spot by a new insight into life. She could not take her eyes from the face of the young man. She forgot that she was staying, forgot that she was staring. She could no more control the swelling thoughts of horror that surged over her and took possession of her than she could have controlled a mob if it had suddenly swept down upon her.

The gates presently lifted silently to let the little procession pass over to her side of the tracks, and within a few short minutes the special train that was to bear the men away to camp came rattling up, laden with other victims of the chance that sent some men on ahead to be pioneers in the camps.

There were a noisy jolly bunch. Perhaps, having had their own sad partings they were only trying to brace themselves against the scenes of other partings through which they must pass all the way along the line. They must be reminded of their own mothers and sisters and sweethearts. Something of this Ruth Macdonald seemed to define to herself as, startled and annoyed by the clamor of the strangers in the midst of the sacredness of the moment, she turned to look at the crowding heads in the car windows and caught the eye of an irrepressible youth:

"Think of me over there!" he shouted, waving a flippant hand and twinkling his eyes at the beautiful girl in her car.

Another time Ruth would have resented such familiarity, but now something touched her spirit with an inexpressible pity, and she let a tiny ripple of a smile pass over her lovely face as her eyes traveled on down the platform in search of the tall form of John Cameron. In the moment of the oncoming train she had somehow lost sight of him. Ah! There he was stooping over a little white haired woman, taking her tenderly in his arms to kiss her. The girl's eyes lingered on him. His whole attitude was such a revelation of the man the rollicking boy had become. It seemed to pleasantly round out her thought of him.

The whistle sounded, the drafted men gave one last wringing hand-clasp, one last look, and sprang on board.

John Cameron was the last to board the train. He stood on the lower step of the last car as it began to move slowly. His hat was lifted, and he stood with slightly lifted chin and eyes that looked as if they had sounded the depths of all sadness and surrendered himself to whatever had been decreed. There was settled sorrow in all the lines of his fine face. Ruth was startled by the change in it; by the look of the boy in the man. Had the war done that for him just in one short summer? Had it done that for the thousands who were going to fight for her? And she was sitting in her luxurious car with a bundle of wool at her feet, and presuming to bear her part by mere knitting! Poor little useless woman that she was! A thing to send a man forth from everything he counted dear or wanted to do, into suffering and hardship—and *death*—perhaps! She shuddered as she watched his face with its strong uplifted look, and its unutterable sorrow. She had not thought he could look like that! Oh, he would be gay to-morrow, like the rest, of course, with his merry jest and his contagious grin, and making light of the serious business of war! He would not be the boy he used to be without the ability to do that. But she would never forget how he had looked in this farewell minute while he was gazing his last on the life of his boyhood and being borne away into a dubious future. She felt a hopelessly yearning, as if, had there been time, she would have liked to have told him how much she appreciated his doing this great deed for her and for all her sisters!

Has it ever been fully explained why the eyes of one person looking hard across a crowd will draw the eyes of another?

The train had slipped along ten feet or more and was gaining speed when John Cameron's eyes met those of Ruth Macdonald, and her vivid speaking face flashed its message to his soul. A pleased wonder sprang into his eyes, a question as his glance lingered, held by the tumult in her face, and the unmistakable personality of her glance. Then his face lit up with its old smile, graver, oh, much! and more deferential than it used to be, with a certain courtliness in it that spoke of maturity of spirit. He lifted his hat a little higher and waved it just a trifle in recognition of her greeting, wondering in sudden confusion if he were really not mistaken after all and had perhaps been appropriating a farewell that belonged to someone else; then amazed and pleased at the flutter of her handkerchief in reply.

The train was moving rapidly now in the midst of a deep throaty cheer that sounded more like a sob, and still he stood on that bottom step with his hat lifted and let his eyes linger on the slender girlish figure in the car, with the morning sun glinting across her red-gold hair, and the beautiful soft rose color in her cheeks.

As the train swept past the little shelter shed he bethought himself and turned a farewell tender smile on the white-haired woman who stood watching him through a mist of tears. Then his eyes went back for one last glimpse of the girl; and so he flashed out of sight around the curve.

3

IT had taken only a short time after all. The crowd drowned its cheer in one deep gasp of silence and broke up tearfully into little groups beginning to melt away at the sound of Michael ringing up the gates, and telling the cars and wagons to hurry that it was almost time for the up-train.

Ruth Macdonald started her car and tried to bring her senses back to their normal calm wondering what had happened to her and why there was such an inexpressible mingling of loss and pleasure in her heart.

The way at first was intricate with congestion of traffic and Ruth was obliged to go slowly. As the road cleared before her she was about to glide forward and make up for lost time. Suddenly a bewildered little woman with white hair darted in front of the car, hesitated, drew back, came on again. Ruth stopped the car shortly, much shaken with the swift vision of catastrophe, and the sudden recognition of the woman. It was the same one who had been with John Cameron.

"Oh, I'm so sorry I startled you!" she called pleasantly,

leaning out of the car. "Won't you get in, please, and let me take you home?"

The woman looked up and there were great tears in her eyes. It was plain why she had not seen where she was going.

"Thank you, no, I couldn't!" she said with a choke in her voice and another blur of tears, "I—you see—I want to get away—I've been seeing off my boy!"

"I know!" said Ruth with quick sympathy, "I saw. And you want to get home quickly and cry. I feel that way myself. But you see I didn't have anybody there and I'd like to do a little something just to be in it. Won't you please get in? You'll get home sooner if I take you; and see! We're blocking the way!"

The woman cast a frightened glance about and assented:

"Of course. I didn't realize!" she said climbing awkwardly in and sitting bolt upright as uncomfortable as could be in the luxurious car beside the girl. It was all too plain she did not wish to be there.

Ruth manoeuvred her car quickly out of the crowd and into a side street, gliding from there to the avenue. She did not speak until they had left the melting crowd well behind them. Then she turned timidly to the woman:

"You—are—his—*mother?*"

She spoke the words hesitatingly as if she feared to touch a wound. The woman's eyes suddenly filled again and a curious little quiver came on the strong chin.

"Yes," she tried to say and smothered the word in her handkerchief pressed quickly to her lips in an effort to control them.

Ruth laid a cool little touch on the woman's other hand that lay in her lap:

"Please forgive me!" she said, "I wasn't sure. I know it must be awful,—cruel—for you!"

"He—is all I have left!" the woman breathed with a quick controlled gasp, "but, of course—it was—right that he should go!"

She set her lips more firmly and blinked off at the blurr of pretty homes on her right without seeing any of them.

"He would have gone sooner, only he thought he ought not to leave me till he had to," she said with another proud little quiver in her voice, as if having once spoken she must go on and say more, "I kept telling him I would get on all right—but he always was so careful of me—ever since his father died!"

"Of course!" said Ruth tenderly turning her face away to struggle with a strange smarting sensation in her own eyes and throat. Then in a low voice she added:

"I knew him, you know. I used to go to the same school with him when I was a little bit of a girl."

The woman looked up with a quick searching glance and brushed the tears away firmly.

"Why, aren't you Ruth Macdonald? *Miss* Macdonald, I mean—excuse me! You live in the big house on the hill, don't you?"

"Yes, I'm Ruth Macdonald. Please don't call me Miss. I'm only nineteen and I still answer to my little girl name," Ruth answered with a charming smile.

The woman's gaze softened.

"I didn't know John knew you," she said speculatively. "He never mentioned—"

"Of course not!" said the girl anticipating, "he wouldn't. It was a long time ago when I was seven and I doubt if he remembers me any more. They took me out of the public school the next year and sent me to St. Mary's for which I've never quite forgiven them, for I'm sure I should have got on much faster at the public school and I loved it. But I've not forgotten the good times I had there, and John was always good to the little girls. We all liked him. I haven't seen him much lately, but I should think he would have grown to be just what you say he is. He looks that way."

Again the woman's eyes searched her face, as if she questioned the sincerity of her words; then apparently satisfied she turned away with a sigh:

"I'd have liked him to know a girl like you," she said wistfully.

"Thank you!" said Ruth brightly, "that sounds like a real compliment. Perhaps we shall know each other yet some day if fortune favors us. I'm quite sure he's worth knowing."

"Oh, he is!" said the little mother, her tears brimming over again and flowing down her dismayed cheeks, "he's quite worth the best society there is, but I haven't been able to manage a lot of things for him. It hasn't been always easy to get along since his father died. Something happened to our money. But anyway, he got through college!" with a flash of triumph in her eyes.

"Wasn't that fine!" said Ruth with sparkling eyes, "I'm sure he's worth a lot more than some of the fellows who have always had every whim gratified. Now, which street? You'll have to tell me. I'm ashamed to say I don't know this part of town very well. Isn't it pretty down here? This house? What a wonderful clematis! I never saw such a wealth of bloom."

"Yes, John planted that and fussed over it," said his mother with pride as she slipped unaccustomedly out of the car to the sidewalk. "I'm very glad to have met you and it was most kind of you to bring me home. To tell the truth"—with a roguish smile that reminded Ruth of her son's grin—"I was so weak and trembling with saying good-bye and trying to keep up so John wouldn't know it, that I didn't know how I was to get home. Though I'm afraid I was a bit discourteous. I couldn't bear the thought of talking to a stranger just then. But you haven't been like a stranger—knowing him, and all—"

"Oh, thank you!" said Ruth, "it's been so pleasant. Do you know, I don't believe I ever realized what an awful thing the war is till I saw those people down at the station this morning saying good-bye. I never realized either what a useless thing I am. I haven't even anybody very dear to send. I can only knit."

"Well, that's a good deal. Some of us haven't time to do that. I never have a minute."

"You don't need to, you've given your son," said Ruth flashing a glance of glorified understanding at the woman.

A beautiful smile came out on the tired sorrowful face.

"Yes, I've given him," she said, "but I'm hoping God will give him back again some day. Do you think that's too much to hope? He is such a good boy!"

"Of course not," said Ruth sharply with a sudden sting of apprehension in her soul. And then she remembered that she had no very intimate acquaintance with God. She wished she might be on speaking terms, at least, and she would go and present a plea for this lonely woman. If it were only Captain La Rue, her favorite cousin, or even the President, she might consider it. But God! She shuddered. Didn't God let this awful war be? Why did He do it? She had never thought much about God before.

"I wish you would let me come to see you sometime and take you for another ride," she said sweetly.

"It would be beautiful!" said the older woman,

"if you would care to take the time from your own friends."

"I would love to have you for one of my friends," said the girl gracefully.

The woman smiled wistfully.

"I'm only here holidays and evenings," she conceded, "I'm doing some government work now."

"I shall come," said Ruth brightly. "I've enjoyed you ever so much." Then she started her car and whirled away into the sunshine.

"She won't come, of course," said the woman to herself as she stood looking mournfully after the car, reluctant to go into the empty house. "I wish she would! Isn't she just like a flower! How wonderful it would be if things had been different, and there hadn't been any war, and my boy could have had her for a friend! Oh!"

Down at the Club House the women waited for the fair young member who had charge of the wool. They rallied her joyously as she hurried in, suddenly aware that she had kept them all waiting.

"I saw her in the crowd at the station this morning," called out Mrs. Pryor, a large placid tease with a twinkle in her eye. "She was picking out the handsomest man for the next sweater she knits. Which one did you choose, Miss Ruth? Tell us. Are you going to write him a letter and stick it in the toe of his sock?"

The annoyed color swept into Ruth's face, but she paid no other heed as she went about her morning duties, preparing the wool to give out. A thought had stolen into her heart that made a tumult there and would not bear turning over even in her mind in the presence of all these curious people. She put it resolutely by as she taught newcomers how to turn the heel of a sock, but now and then it crept back again and was the cause of her dropping an occasional stitch.

Dottie Wetherill came to find out what was the matter

with her sock, and to giggle and gurgle about her brother Bob and his friends. Bob, it appeared, was going to bring five officers home with him next week end and they were to have a dance Saturday night. Of course Ruth must come. Bob was soon to get his *first* lieutenant's commission. There had been a mistake, of course, or he would have had it before this, some favoritism shown; but now Bob had what they called a "pull," and things were going to be all right for him. Bob said you couldn't get anywhere without a "pull." And didn't Ruth think Bob looked perfectly fine in his uniform?

It annoyed Ruth to hear such talk and she tried to make it plain to Dottie that she was mistaken about "pull." There was no such thing. It was all imagination. She knew, for her cousin, Captain La Rue, was very close to the Government and he had told her so. He said that real worth was always recognized, and that it didn't make any difference where it was found or who your friends were. It mattered *what you were*.

She fixed Dottie's sock and moved on to the wool table to get ready an allotment for some of the ladies to take home.

Mrs. Wainwright bustled in, large and florid and well groomed, with a bunch of photographer's proofs of her son Harry in his uniform. She called loudly for Ruth to come and inspect them. There were some twenty or more poses, each one seemingly fatter, more pompous and conceited looking than the last. She stated in boisterous good humor that Harry particularly wanted Ruth's opinion before he gave the order. At that Mrs. Pryor bent her head to her neighbor and nodded meaningly, as if a certain matter of discussion were settled now beyond all question. Ruth caught the look and its meaning and the color flooded her face once more, much to her annoyance. She wondered angrily if she would never be able to stop that childish habit of blushing, and why it annoyed her so very much this morning to have her name coupled with that of Harry Wainwright. He was her old friend and playmate, having lived next door to her all her life, and it was but natural when everybody was sweethearting and getting married, that people should speak of her and wonder whether there might be anything more to their relationship than mere friendship. Still it annoyed her. Continually as she turned the pages from one fat smug Wainwright countenance to another, she saw in a mist the face of another man, with uplifted head and sorrowful eyes. She wondered if when the time came for Harry Wainwright to go he would have aught of the vision, and aught of the holiness of sorrow that had shown in that other face.

She handed the proofs back to the mother, so like her son in her ample blandness, and wondered if Mrs. Cameron would have a picture of her son in his uniform, fine and large and lifelike as these were.

She interrupted her thoughts to hear Mrs. Wainwright's clarion voice lifted in parting from the door of the Club House on her way back to her car:

"Well, good-bye, Ruth dear. Don't hesitate to let me know if you'd like to have either of the other two large ones for your own 'specials,' you know. I shan't mind changing the order a bit. Harry said you were to have as many as you wanted. I'll hold the proofs for a day or two and let you think it over."

Ruth lifted her eyes to see the gaze of every woman in the room upon her, and for a moment she felt as if she almost hated poor fat doting Mamma Wainwright. Then the humorous side of the moment came to help her and her face blossomed into a smile as she jauntily replied:

"Oh, no, please don't bother, Mrs. Wainwright. I'm not going to paper the wall with them. I have other friends, you know. I think your choice was the best of them all."

Then as gaily as if she were not raging within her soul she turned to help poor Dottie Wetherill who was hopelessly muddled about turning her heel.

Dottie chattered on above the turmoil of her soul, and her words were as tiny April showers sizzling on a red hot cannon. By and by she picked up Dottie's dropped stitches. After all, what did such things matter when there was *war* and men were giving their *lives!*

"And Bob says he doubts if they ever get to France. He says he thinks the war will be over before half the men get trained. He says, for his part, he'd like the trip over after the submarines have been put out of business. It would be something to tell about, don't you know? But Bob thinks the war will be over soon. Don't you think so, Ruth?"

"I don't know what I think," said Ruth exasperated at the little prattler. It seemed so awful for a girl with brains—or hadn't she brains?—to chatter on interminably in that inane fashion about a matter of such awful portent. And yet perhaps the child was only trying to cover up her fears, for she all too evidently worshipped her brother.

Ruth was glad when at last the morning was over and one by one the women gathered their belongings together and went home. She stayed longer than the rest to put the work in order. When they were all gone she drove around by the way of the post office and asked the old post master who had been there for twenty years and knew everybody, if he could tell her the address of the boys who had gone to camp that morning. He wrote it down and she tucked it in her blouse saying she thought the Red Cross would be sending them something soon. Then she drove thoughtfully away to her beautiful sheltered home, where the thought of war hardly dared to enter yet in any but a playful form. But somehow everything was changed within the heart of Ruth Macdonald and she looked about on all the familiar places with new eyes. What right had she to be living here in all this luxury while over there men were dying every day that she might live?

4

THE sun shone blindly over the broad dusty drill-field. The men marched and wheeled, about-faced and counter-marched in their new olive-drab uniforms and thought of home—those that had any homes to think about. Some who did not thought of a home that might have been if this war had not happened.

There were times when their souls could rise to the great occasion and their enthusiasm against the foe could carry them to all lengths of joyful sacrifice, but this was not one of the times. It was a breathless Indian summer morning, and the dust was inches thick. It rose like a soft yellow mist over the mushroom city of forty thousand men, brought into being at the command of a Nation's leader. Dust lay like a fine yellow powder over everything. An approaching company looked like a cloud as it drew near. One could scarcely see the men near by for the cloud of yellow dust everywhere.

The water was bad this morning when every man was thirsty. It had been boiled for safety and was served warm and tasted of disinfectants. The breakfast had been oatmeal and salty bacon swimming in congealed grease.

The "boy" in the soldier's body was very low indeed that morning. The "man" with his disillusioned eyes had come to the front. Of course this was nothing like the hardships they would have to endure later, but it was enough for the present to their unaccustomed minds, and harder because they were doing nothing that seemed worth while—just marching about and doing sordid duties when they were all eager for the fray and to have it over with. They had begun to see that they were going to have to learn to wait and be patient, to obey blindly; they—who never had brooked commands from any one, most of them, not even from their own parents. They had been free as air, and they had never been tied down to certain company. Here they were all mixed up, college men and foreign laborers, rich and poor, cultured and coarse, clean and defiled, and it went pretty hard with them all. They had come, a bundle of prejudices and wills, and they had first to learn that every prejudice they had been born with or cultivated, must be given up or laid aside. They were not their own. They belonged to a great machine. The great perfect conception of the army as a whole had not yet dawned upon them. They were occupied with unpleasant details in the first experimental stages. At first the discomforts seemed to rise and obliterate even the great object for which they had come, and discontent sat upon their faces.

Off beyond the drill-field whichever way they looked, there were barracks the color of the dust, and long stark roads, new and rough, the color of the barracks, with jitneys and trucks and men like ants crawling furiously back and forth upon them all animated by the same great necessity that had brought the men here. Even the sky seemed yellow like the dust. The trees were gone except at the edges of the camp, cut down to make way for more barracks, in even ranks like men.

Out beyond the barracks mimic trenches were being dug, and puppets hung in long lines for mock enemies. There were skeleton bridges to cross, walls to scale, embankments to jump over, and all, everything, was that awful olive-drab color till the souls of the new-made soldiers cried out within them for a touch of scarlet or green or blue to relieve the dreary monotony. Sweat and dust and grime, weariness, homesickness, humbled pride, these were the tales of the first days of those men gathered from all quarters who were pioneers in the first camps.

Corporal Cameron marched his awkward squad back and forth, through all the various manoeuvres, again and again, giving his orders in short, sharp tones, his face set, his heart tortured with the thought of the long months and years of this that might be before him. The world seemed most unfriendly to him these days. Not that it had ever been over kind, yet always before his native wit and happy temperament had been able to buoy him up and carry him through hopefully. Now, however, hope seemed gone. This war might last till he was too old to carry out any of his dreams and pull himself out of the place where fortune had dropped him. Gradually one thought had been shaping itself clearly out of the days he had spent in camp. This life on earth was not all of existence. There must be something bigger beyond. It wasn't sane and sensible to think that any God would allow such waste of humanity as to let some suffer all the way through with nothing beyond to compensate. There was a meaning to the suffering. There must be. It must be a preparation for something beyond, infinitely better and more worth while. What was it and how should he learn the meaning of his own particular bit?

John Cameron had never thought about religion before in his life. He had believed in a general way in a

God, or thought he believed, and that a book called the Bible told about Him and was the authentic place to learn how to be good. The doubts of the age had not touched him because he had never had any interest in them. In the ordinary course of events he might never have thought about them in relation to himself until he came to die—perhaps not then. In college he had been too much engrossed with other things to listen to the arguments, or to be influenced by the general atmosphere of unbelief. He had been a boy whose inner thoughts were kept under lock and key, and who had lived his heart life absolutely alone, although his rich wit and bubbling merriment had made him a general favorite where pure fun among the fellows was going. He loved to "rough house" as he called it, and his boyish pranks had always been the talk of the town, the envied of the little boys; but no one knew his real, serious thoughts. Not even his mother, strong and self-repressed like himself, had known how to get down beneath the surface and commune with him. Perhaps she was afraid or shy.

Now that he was really alone among all this mob of men of all sorts and conditions, he had retired more and more into the inner sanctuary of self and tried to think out the meaning of life. From the chaos that reigned in his mind he presently selected a few things that he called "facts" from which to work. These were "God, Hereafter, Death." These things he must reckon with. He had been working on a wrong hypothesis all his life. He had been trying to live for this world as if it were the end and aim of existence, and now this war had come and this world had suddenly melted into chaos. It appeared that he and thousands of others must probably give up their part in this world before they had hardly tried it, if they would set things right again for those that should come after. But, even if he had lived out his ordinary years in peace and success, and had all that life could give him, it would not have lasted long, seventy years or so, and what were they after they were past? No, there was something beyond or it all wouldn't have been made—this universe with the carefully thought out details working harmoniously one with another. It wouldn't have been worth while otherwise. There would have been no reason for a heart life.

There were boys and men in the army who thought otherwise. Who had accepted this life as being all. Among these were the ones who when they found they were taken in the draft and must go to camp, had spent their last three weeks of freedom drunk because they wanted to get all the "fun" they could out of life that was left to them. They were the men who were plunging into all the sin they could find before they went away to fight because they felt they had but a little time to live and what did it matter? But John Cameron was not one of these. His soul would not let him alone until he had thought it all out, and he had come thus far with these three facts, "God, Death, A Life Hereafter." He turned these over in his mind for days and then he changed their order, *"Death, A Life Hereafter, God."*

Death was the grim person he was going forth to meet one of these days or months on the field of France or Italy, or somewhere "over there." He was not to wait for Death to come and get him as had been the old order. This was WAR and he was going out to challenge Death. He was convinced that whether Death was a servant of God or the Devil, in some way it would make a difference with his own personal life hereafter, how he met Death. He was not satisfied with just meeting Death bravely, with the ardor of patriotism in his breast, as he heard so many about him talk in these days. That was well so far as it went, but it did not solve the mystery of the future life nor make him sure how he would stand in that other world to which Death stood ready to escort him presently. Death might be victor over his body, but he wanted to be sure that Death should not also kill that something within him which he felt must live forever. He turned it over for days and came to the conclusion that the only one who could help him was God. God was the beginning of it all. If there was a God He must be available to help a soul in a time like this. There must be a way to find God and get the secret of life, and so be ready to meet Death that Death should not conquer anything but the body. How could one find God? Had anybody ever found Him? Did anyone really *think* they had found Him? These were questions that beat in upon his soul day after day as he drilled his men and went through the long hard hours of discipline, or lay upon his straw tick at night while a hundred and fifty other men about him slept.

His mother's secret attempts at religion had been too feeble and too hidden in her own breast to have made much of an impression upon him. She had only *hoped* her faith was founded upon a rock. She had not *known*. And so her buffeted soul had never given evidence to her son of hidden holy refuge where he might flee with her in time of need.

Now and then the vision of a girl blurred across his thoughts uncertainly, like a bright moth hovering in the distance whose shadow fell across his dusty path. But it was far away and vague, and only a glance in her eyes belonged to him. She was not of his world.

He looked up to the yellow sky through the yellow dust, and his soul cried out to find the way to God before he had to meet Death, but the heavens seemed like molten brass. Not that he was afraid of death with a

physical fear, but that his soul recoiled from being con-
quered by it and he felt convinced that there was a way
to meet it with a smile of assurance if only he could find
it out. He had read that people had met it that way. Was
it all their imagination? The mere illusion of a fanatical
brain? Well, he would try to find out God. He would
put himself in the places where God ought to be, and
when he saw any indication that God was there he
would cry out until he made God hear him!

The day he came to that conclusion was Sunday and
he went over to the Y.M.C.A. Auditorium. They were
having a Mary Pickford moving picture show there. If
he had happened to go at any time during the morning
he might have heard some fine sermons and perhaps
have found the right man to help him, but this was
evening and the men were being amused.

He stood for a few moments and watched the pretty
show. The sunlight on Mary's beautiful hair, as it fell
glimmering through the trees in the picture reminded
him of the red-gold lights on Ruth Macdonald's hair the
morning he left home, and with a sigh he turned away
and walked to the edge of camp where the woods were
still standing.

Alone he looked up to the starry sky. Amusement was
not what he wanted now. He was in search of something
vague and great that would satisfy, and give him a reason
for being and suffering and dying perhaps. He called it
God because he had no other name for it. Red-gold hair
might be for others but not for him. He might not take
it where he would and he would not take it where it lay
easy to get. If he had been in the same class with some
other fellows he knew he would have wasted no time on
follies. He would have gone for the very highest, finest
woman. But there! What was the use! Besides, even if
he had been—and he had had—every joy of life here was

but a passing show and must sometime come to an end. And at the end would be this old problem. Sometime he would have had to realize it, even if war had not come and brought the revelation prematurely. What was it that he wanted? How could he find out how to die? Where was God?

But the stars were high and cold and gave no answer, and the whispering leaves, although they soothed him, sighed and gave no help.

The feeling was still with him next morning when the mail was distributed. There would be nothing for him. His mother had written her weekly letter and it had reached him the day before. He could expect nothing for several days now. Other men were getting sheaves of letters. How friendless he seemed among them all. One had a great chocolate cake that a girl had sent him and the others were crowding around to get a bit. It was doubtful if the laughing owner got more than a bite himself. He might have been one of the group if he had chosen. They all liked him well enough, although they knew him very little as yet, for he had kept much to himself. But he turned sharply away from them and went out. Somehow he was not in the mood for fun. He felt he must be growing morbid but he could not throw it off that morning. It all seemed so hopeless, the things he had tried to do in life and the slow progress he had made upward; and now to have it all blocked by war!

None of the other fellows ever dreamed that he was lonely, big, husky, handsome fellow that he was, with a continuous joke on his lips for those he had chosen as associates, with an arm of iron and a jaw that set like steel, grim and unmistakably brave. The awkward squad as they wrathfully obeyed his stern orders would have told you he had no heart, the way he worked them, and would not have believed that he was just plain homesick and lonesome for some one to care for him.

He was not hungry that day when the dinner call came, and flung himself down under a scrub oak outside the barracks while the others rushed in with their mess kits ready for beans or whatever was provided for them. He was glad that they were gone, glad that he might have the luxury of being miserable all alone for a few minutes. He felt strangely as if he were going to cry, and yet he didn't know what about. Perhaps he was going to be sick. That would be horrible down in that half finished hospital with hardly any equipment yet! He must brace up and put an end to such softness. It was all in the idea anyway.

Then a great hand came down upon his shoulder with a mighty slap and he flung himself bolt upright with a frown to find his comrade whose bunk was next to his in the barracks. He towered over Cameron polishing his tin plate with a vigor.

"What's the matter with you, you boob? There's roast beef and its good. Cooky saved a piece for you. I told him you'd come. Go in and get it quick! There's a letter for you, too, in the office. I'd have brought it only I was afraid I would miss you. Here, take my mess kit and hurry! There's some cracker-jack pickles, too, little sweet ones! Step lively, or some one will swipe them all!"

Cameron arose, accepted his friend's dishes and sauntered into the mess hall. The letter couldn't be very important. His mother had no time to write again soon, and there was no one else. It was likely an advertisement or a formal greeting from some of the organizations at home. They did that about fortnightly, the Red Cross, the Woman's Club, The Emergency Aid, The Fire Company. It was kind in them but he wasn't keen about it just then. It could wait until he got his dinner. They didn't have roast beef every day, and now that he thought about it he was hungry.

He almost forgot the letter after dinner until a comrade reminded him, handing over a thick delicately scented envelope with a silver crest on the back. The boys got off their kidding about "the girl he'd left behind him" and he answered with his old good-natured grin that made them love him, letting them think he had all kinds of girls, for the dinner had somewhat restored his spirits, but he crumpled the letter into his pocket and got away into the woods to read it.

Deliberately he walked down the yellow road, up over the hill by the signal corps tents, across Wig-Wag Park to the woods beyond, and sat down on a log with his letter. He told himself that it was likely one of those fool letters the fellows were getting all the time from silly girls who were uniform-crazy. He wouldn't answer it, of course, and he felt a kind of contempt with himself for being weak enough to read it even to satisfy his curiosity.

Then he tore open the envelope half angrily and a faint whiff of violets floated out to him. Over his head a meadow lark trilled a long sweet measure, and glad surprise suddenly entered into his soul.

5

THE letter was written in a fine beautiful hand and even
before he saw the silver monogram at the top, he knew
who was the writer, though he did not even remember
to have seen the writing before:

My Dear Friend:

I have hesitated a long time before writing because I do not know that I have the right to call
you a friend, or even an acquaintance in the com-
monly accepted sense of that term. It is so long
since you and I went to school together, and we
have been so widely separated since then that
perhaps you do not even remember me, and may
consider my letter an intrusion. I hope not, for I
should hate to rank with the girls who are writing
to strangers under the license of mistaken patriotism.

My reason for writing you is that a good many
years ago you did something very nice and kind for
me one day, in fact you helped me twice, although
I don't suppose you knew it. Then the other day,

when you were going to camp and I sat in my car and watched you, it suddenly came over me that you were doing it again; this time a great big wonderful thing for me; and doing it just as quietly and inconsequentially as you did it before; and all at once I realized how splendid it was and wanted to thank you.

It came over me, too, that I had never thanked you for the other times, and very likely you never dreamed that you had done anything at all.

You see I was only a little girl, very much frightened, because Chuck Woodcock had teased me about my curls and said that he was going to catch me and cut them off, and send me home to my aunt that way, and she would turn me out of the house. He had been frightening me for several days, so that I was afraid to go to school alone, and yet I would not tell my aunt because I was afraid she would take me away from the Public School and send me to a Private School which I did not want. But that day I had seen Chuck Woodcock steal in behind the hedge, ahead of the girls. The others were ahead of me and I was all out of breath—running to catch up because I was afraid to pass him alone; and just as I got near two of them,—Mary Wurts and Caroline Meadows, you remember them, don't you?—they gave a scream and pitched headlong on the sidewalk. They had tripped over a wire he had stretched from the tree to the hedge. I stopped short and got behind a tree, and I remember how the tears felt in my throat, but I was afraid to let them out because Chuck would call me a cry-baby and I hated that. And just then you came along behind me and jumped through the hedge and caught Chuck and gave him an awful whipping. "Licking" I believe we called it then. I remember how condemned I felt as I ran by the hedge and knew in my heart that I was glad you were hurting him because he had been so cruel to me. He used to pull my curls whenever he sat behind me in recitation.

I remember you came in to school late with your hair all mussed up beautifully, and a big tear in your coat, and a streak of mud on your face. I was so worried lest the teacher would find out you had been fighting and make you stay after school. Because you see I knew in my heart that you had been winning a battle for me, and if anybody had to stay after school I wished it could be me because of what you had done for me. But you came in laughing as you always did, and looking as if nothing in the world unusual had happened, and when you passed my desk you threw before me the loveliest pink rose bud I ever saw. That was the second thing you did for me.

Perhaps you won't understand how nice that was, either, for you see you didn't know how unhappy I had been. The girls hadn't been very friendly with me. They told me I was "stuck up," and they said I was too young to be in their classes anyway and ought to go to Kindergarten. It was all very hard for me because I longed to be big and have them for my friends. I was very lonely in that great big house with only my aunt and grandfather for company. But the girls wouldn't be friends at all until they saw you give me that rose, and that turned the tide. They were crazy about you, every one of them, and they made up to me after that and told me their secrets and shared their lunch and we had great times. And it was all because you gave me the rose that day. The rose itself was lovely and I was tremendously happy over it for its own sake, but it meant a whole lot to me besides, and opened the little world of school to my longing feet. I always wanted to thank you for it, but you looked as if you didn't want me to, so I never dared; and lately I wasn't quite sure you knew me, because you never looked my way any more.

But when I saw you standing on the platform the other day with the other drafted men, it all came over me how you were giving up the life you had planned to go out and fight for me and other girls like me. I hadn't thought of the war that way before, although, of course, I had heard that thought expressed in speeches; but it never struck into my heart until I saw the look on your face. It was a kind of "knightliness," if there is such a word, and when I thought about it I realized it was the very same look you had worn when you burst through the hedge after Chuck Woodcock, and again when you came back and threw that rose on my desk. Although, you had a big, broad boy's-grin on your face then, and were chewing gum I remember quite distinctly; and the other day you looked so serious and sorry as if it meant a great deal to you to go, but you were giving up everything gladly without even thinking of hesitating. The look on your face was a man's look, not a boy's.

It has meant so much to me to realize this last great thing that you are doing for me and for the other girls of our country that I had to write and tell you how much I appreciate it.

I have been wondering whether some one has been knitting you a sweater yet, and the other things that they knit for soldiers; and if they haven't, whether you would let me send them to you? It is the only thing I can do for you who have done so much for me.

I hope you will not think I am presuming to have written this on the strength of a childish acquaintance. I wish you all honors that can come to you on such a quest as yours, and I had almost said all good luck, only that word sounds too frivolous and pagan for such a serious matter; so I will say all safety for a swift accomplishment of your task and a swift homecoming. I used to think when I was a little child that nothing could ever hurt you or make you afraid, and I cannot help feeling now that you will come through the fire unscathed. May I hope to hear from you about the sweater and things? And may I sign myself

Your friend?
Ruth Macdonald

John Cameron lifted his eyes from the paper at last and looked up at the sky. Had it ever been so blue before? At the trees. What whispering wonders of living green! Was that only a bird that was singing that heavenly song—a meadow lark, not an angel? Why had he never appreciated meadow larks before?

He rested his head back against a big oak and his soldier's hat fell off on the ground. He closed his eyes and the burden of loneliness that had borne down upon him all these weeks in the camp lifted from his heart. Then he tried to realize what had come to him. Ruth Macdonald, the wonder and admiration of his childhood days, the admired and envied of the home town, the petted beauty at whose feet every man fell, the girl who had everything that wealth could purchase! She had remembered the little old rose he had dared to throw on her desk, and had bridged the years with this letter!

He was carried back in spirit to the day he left for camp. To the look in her eyes as he moved away on the train. The look had been real then, and not just a fleeting glance helped out by his fevered imagination. There had been true friendliness in her eyes. She had intended to say good-bye to him! She had put him on a level with her own beautiful self. She had knighted him, as it were, and sent him forth! Even the war had become different since she chose to think he was going forth to fight her battles. What a sacred trust!

Afar in the distance a bugle sounded that called to duty. He had no idea how the time had flown. He glanced at his wrist watch and was amazed. He sprang to his feet and strode over the ground, but the way no longer seemed dusty and blinded with sunshine. It shone like a path of glory before his willing feet, and he went to his afternoon round of duties like a new man. He had a friend, a real friend, one that he had known a long time. There was no fear that she was just writing to him to get one more soldier at her feet as some girls would have done. Her letter was too frank and sincere to leave a single doubt about what she meant. He would take her at her word.

Sometime during the course of the afternoon it occurred to him to look at the date of the letter, and he found to his dismay that it had been written nearly four weeks before and had been travelling around through various departments in search of him, because it had not the correct address. He readily guessed that she had not wanted to ask for his company and barracks; she would not have known who to ask. She did not know his mother, and who else was there? His old companions were mostly gone to France or camp somewhere.

And now, since all this time had elapsed she would think he had not cared, had scorned her letter or thought it unmaidenly! He was filled with dismay and anxiety lest he had hurt her frankness by his seeming indifference. And the knitted things, the wonderful things that she had made with her fair hands! Would she have given them to some one else by this time? Of course, it meant little to her save as a kind of acknowledgment for something she thought he had done for her as a child, but they meant so much to him! Much more than they ought to do, he knew, for he was in no position to allow himself to become deeply attached to even the handiwork of any girl in her position. However, nobody need ever know how much he cared, had always cared, for the lovely little girl with her blue eyes, her long curls, her shy sweet smile and modest ways, who had seemed to him like an angel from heaven when he was a boy. She had said he did not know that he was helping her when he burst through the hedge on the cowering Chuck Woodcock; and he would likely never dare to tell her that it was because he saw her fright and saw her hide behind that tree that he went to investigate and so was able to administer a just punishment. He had picked that rose from the extreme west corner of a great petted rose bush on the Wainwright lawn, reaching through an elaborate iron fence to get it as he went cross-lots back to school. He would call it stealing now to do that same, but then it had been in the nature of a holy rite offered to a vestal virgin. Yet he must have cast it down with the grin of an imp, boorish urchin that he was; and he remembered blushing hotly in the dark afterwards at his presumption, as he thought of it alone at night. And all the time she had been liking it. The little girl—the little sweet girl! She had kept it in her heart and remembered it!

His heart was light as air as he went back to the

barracks for retreat. A miracle had been wrought for him which changed everything. No, he was not presuming on a friendly letter. Maybe there would be fellows who would think there wasn't much in just a friendly letter to a lonely soldier, and a sweater or two more or less. But then they would never have known what it was to be so lonely for friendship, real friendship, as he was.

He would hurry through supper and get to the Y.M.C.A. hut to write her an answer. He would explain how the letter had been delayed and say he hoped she had not given the things away to someone else. He began planning sentences as he stood at attention during the captain's inspection at retreat. Somehow the captain was tiresomely particular about the buttons and pocket flaps and little details to-night. He waited impatiently for the command to break ranks, and was one of the first at the door of the mess hall waiting for supper, his face alight, still planning what he would say in that letter and wishing he could get some fine stationery to write upon; wondering if there was any to be had with his caduces on it.

At supper he bubbled with merriment. An old school-mate might have thought him rejuvenated. He wore his schoolboy grin and rattled off puns and jokes, keeping the mess hall in a perfect roar.

At last he was out in the cool of the evening with the wonderful sunset off in the west, on his way to the Y.M.C.A. hut. He turned a corner swinging into the main road and there, coming toward him, not twenty feet away, he saw Lieutenant Wainwright!

6

THERE was no possible way to avoid meeting him. John Cameron knew that with the first glance. He also knew that Wainwright had recognized him at once and was lifting his chin already with that peculiar, disagreeable tilt of triumph that had always been so maddening to one who knew the small mean nature of the man.

Of course, there was still time to turn deliberately about and flee in the other direction, but that would be all too obvious, and an open confession of weakness. John Cameron was never at any time a coward.

His firm lips set a trifle more sternly than usual, his handsome head was held high with fine military bearing. He came forward without faltering for even so much as the fraction of a waver. There was not a flicker in his eyes set straight ahead. One would never have known from his looks that he recognized the oncoming man, or had so much as realized that an officer was approaching, yet his brain was doing some rapid calculation. He had said in his heart if not openly that he would never salute this man. He had many times in their home town openly passed him without salute because he had absolutely no respect for him, and felt that he owed it to his sense of the fitness of things not to give him deference, but that was a different matter from camp. He knew that Wainwright was in a position to do him injury, and no longer stood in fear of a good thrashing from him as at home, because here he could easily have the offender put in the guard house and disgraced forever. Nothing, of course, would delight him more than thus to humiliate his sworn enemy. Yet Cameron walked on knowing that he had resolved not to salute him.

It was not merely pride in his own superiority. It was contempt for the nature of the man, for his low contemptible plots and tricks, and cunning ways, for his entire lack of principle, and his utter selfishness and heartlessness, that made Cameron feel justified in his attitude toward Wainwright. "He is nothing but a Hun at heart," he told himself bitterly.

But the tables were turned. Wainwright was no longer in his home town where his detestable pranks had goaded many of his neighbors and fellowtownsmen into a cordial hatred of him. He was in a great military camp, vested with a certain amount of authority, with the right to report those under him; who in turn could not retaliate by telling what they knew of him because it was a court-martial offense for a private to report an officer. Well, naturally the United States was not supposed to have put men in authority who needed reporting. Cameron, of course, realized that these things had to be in order to maintain military discipline. But it was inevitable that some unworthy ones should creep in, and Wainwright was surely one of those unworthy ones. He would not bend to him, officer, or no officer. What did he care what happened to himself? Who was there to care but his mother? And she would understand if the news should happen to penetrate to the home town, which was hardly likely. Those who knew him would not doubt him, those who did not mattered little. There was really no one who would care. Stay! A letter crackled in his breast pocket and a cold chill of horror struggled up from his heart. Suppose *she* should hear of it! Yes, he would care for that!

They were almost meeting now and Cameron's eyes were straight ahead staring hard at the big green shape of the theatre a quarter of a mile away. His face under its usual control showed no sign of the tumult in his heart, which flamed with a sudden despair against a fate that had placed him in such a desperate situation. If there were a just power who controlled the affairs of men, how could it let such things happen to one who had always tried to live an upright life? It seemed for that instant as if all the unfairness and injustice of his own hard life had culminated in that one moment when he would have to do or not do and bear the consequences.

Then suddenly out from the barracks close at hand with brisk step and noble bearing came Captain La Rue, swinging down the walk into the road straight between the two men and stopped short in front of Cameron with a light of real welcome in his eyes, as he lifted his hand to answer the salute which the relieved Cameron instantly flashed at him.

In that second Lieutenant Wainwright flung past them with a curt salute to the higher officer and a glare at the corporal which the latter seemed not to see. It was so simultaneous with Cameron's salute of La Rue that nobody on earth could say that the salute had not included the lieutenant, yet both the lieutenant and the corporal knew that it had not; and Wainwright's brow was dark with intention as he turned sharply up the walk to the barracks which the captain had just left.

"I was just coming in search of you, Cameron," said

the captain with a twinkle in his eyes, and his voice was clearly distinct to Wainwright as he loitered in the barracks doorway to listen, "I went down to Washington yesterday and put in the strongest plea I knew how for your transfer. I hope it will go through all right. There is no one else out for the job and you are just the man for the place. It will be a great comfort to have you with me."

A few more words and the busy man moved on eluding Cameron's earnest thanks and leaving him to pursue his course to the Y.M.C.A. hut with a sense of soothing and comfort. It never occurred to either of them that their brief conversation had been overheard, and would not have disturbed them if it had.

Lieutenant Wainwright lingered on the steps of the barracks with a growing curiosity and satisfaction. The enemy were playing right into his hands: *both* the enemy—for he hated Captain La Rue as sin always hates the light.

He lounged about the barracks in deep thought for a few minutes and then made a careful toilet and went out.

He knew exactly where to go and how to use his influence, which was not small, although not personal. It was characteristic of the man that it made no difference to him that the power he was wielding was a borrowed power whose owner would have been the last man to have done what he was about to do with it. He had never in his life hesitated about getting whatever he wanted by whatever means presented itself. He was often aware that people gave him what he wanted merely to get rid of him, but this did not alloy his pleasure in his achievement.

He was something of a privileged character in the high place to which he betook himself, on account of the supreme regard which was held for the uncle, a mighty automobile king, through whose influence he had obtained his commission. So far he had not availed himself of his privileges too often and had therefore not as yet outworn his welcome, for he was a true diplomat. He entered this evening with just the right shade of delicate assurance and humble affrontery to assure him a cordial welcome and gracefully settled himself into the friendliness that was readily extended to him. He was versed in all the ways of the world and when he chose could put up a good appearance. He knew that for the sake of his father's family and more especially because of his uncle's high standing, this great official whom he was calling upon was bound to be nice to him for a time. So he bided his time till a few other officials had left and his turn came.

The talk was all personal, a few words about his relatives and then questions about himself, his commission, how he liked it, and how things were going with him. Mere form and courtesy, but he knew how to use the conversation for his own ends:

"Oh, I'm getting along fine and dandy!" he declared effusively, "I'm just crazy about camp! I like the life! But I'll tell you what makes me tired. It's these little common guys running around fussing about their jobs and trying to get a lot of pull to get into some other place. Now there's an instance of that in our company, a man from my home town, no account whatever and never was, but he's got it in his head that he's a square peg in a round hole and he wants to be transferred. He shouts about it from morning till night trying to get everybody to help him, and at last I understand he's hoodwinked one captain into thinking he's the salt of the earth, and they are plotting together to get him transferred. I happened to overhear them talking about it just now, how they are going to this one and that one in Washington to get things fixed to suit them. They think they've got the right dope on things all right and it's going through for him to get his transfer. It makes me sick. He's no more fit for a commission than my dog, not as fit, for he could at least obey orders. This fellow never did anything but what he pleased. I've known him since we were kids and never liked him. But he has a way with him that gets people till they understand him. It's too bad when the country needs real men to do their duty that a fellow like that can get a commission when he is utterly inefficient besides being a regular breeder of trouble. But, of course, I can't tell anybody what I know about him."

"I guess you needn't worry, Wainwright. They can't make any transfers without sending them up to me, and you may be good and sure I'm not transferring anybody just now without a good reason, no matter who is asking it. He's in your company, is he? And where does he ask to be transferred? Just give me his name. I'll make a note of it. If it ever comes up I'll know how to finish him pretty suddenly. Though I doubt if it does. People are not pulling wires just now. This is *war* and everything means business. However, if I find there has been wire-pulling I shall know how to deal with it summarily. It's a court-martial offense, you know."

They passed on to other topics, and Wainwright with his little eyes gleaming triumphantly soon took himself out into the starlight knowing that he had done fifteen minutes' good work and not wishing to outdo it. He strolled contendedly back to officers' quarters wearing a more complacent look on his heavy features. He would teach John Cameron to ignore him!

Meantime John Cameron with his head among the stars walked the dusty camp streets and forgot the existence of Lieutenant Wainwright. A glow of gratitude had flooded his soul at sight of his beloved captain, whom he hoped soon to be able to call *his* captain. Unconsciously he walked with more self-respect as the words of confidence and trust rang over again in his ears. Unconsciously the little matters of personal enmity became smaller, of less importance, beside the greater things of life in which he hoped soon to have a real part. If he got this transfer it meant a chance to work with a great man in a great way that would not only help the war but would be of great value to him in this world after the war was over. It was good to have the friendship of a man like that, fine, clean, strong, intellectual, kind, just, human, gentle as a woman, yet stern against all who deviated from the path of right.

The dusk was settling into evening and twinkling lights gloomed out amid the misty, dust-laden air. Snatches of wild song chorused out from open windows:

> *She's my lady, my baby,*
> *She's cock-eyed, she's crazy.*

The twang of a banjo trailed in above the voices, with a sound of scuffling. Loud laughter broke the thread of the song leaving "Mary Ann!" to soar out alone. Then the chorus took it up once more:

> *All her teeth are false*
> *From eating Rochelle salts—*
> *She's my freckle-faced, consumptive*
> *MARY ANN-N-N!*

Cameron turned in at the quiet haven of the Y.M.C.A. hut, glad to leave the babel sounds outside. Somehow they did not fit his mood to-night, although there were times when he could roar the outlandish gibberish with the best of them. But to-night he was on such a wonderful sacred errand bent, that it seemed as though he wanted to keep his soul from contact with rougher things lest somehow it might get out of tune and so unfit him for the task before him.

And then when he had seated himself before the simple desk he looked at the paper with discontent. True, it was all that was provided and it was good enough for ordinary letters, but this letter to her was different. He wished he had something better. To think he was really writing to *her!* And now that he was here with the paper before him what was he to say? Words seemed to have deserted him. How should he address her?

It was not until he had edged over to the end of the bench away from everybody else and taken out the precious letter that he gained confidence and took up his pen:

"My dear friend:—" Why, he would call her his friend, of course, that was what she had called him. And as he wrote he seemed to see her again as she sat in her car by the station the day he started on his long, long trail and their eyes had met. Looking so into her eyes again, he wrote straight from his soul:

My Dear Friend:

Your letter has just reached me after travelling about for weeks. I am not going to try to tell you how wonderful it is to me to have it. In fact, the wonder began that morning I left home when you smiled at me and waved a friendly farewell. It was a great surprise to me. I had not supposed until that moment that you remembered my existence. Why should you? And it has never been from lack of desire to do so that I failed to greet you when we passed in the street. I did not think that I, a mere little hoodlum from your infant days, had a right to intrude upon your grown-up acquaintance without a hint from you that such recognition would be agreeable. I never blamed you for not speaking of course. Perhaps I didn't give you the chance. I simply thought I had grown out of your memory as was altogether natural. It was indeed a pleasant experience to see that light of friendliness in your eyes at the station that day, and to know it was a real personal recognition and not just a patriotic gush of enthusiasm for the whole shabby lot of us draftees starting out to an unknown future. I thanked you in my heart for that little bit of personal friendliness but I never expected to have an opportunity to thank you in words, nor to have the friendliness last after I had gone away. When your letter came this morning it sure was some pleasant surprise. I know you have a great many friends, and plenty of people to write letters to, but somehow there was a real note of comradeship in the one you wrote me, not as if you just felt sorry for me because I had to go off to war and fight and maybe get killed. It was as if the conditions of the times had suddenly swept away a lot of foolish conventions of the world, which may all have their good use perhaps at times, but at a time like this are superfluous, and you had just gravely and sweetly offered me an old friend's sympathy and good will. As such I have taken it and am rejoicing in it.

Don't make any mistake about this, however. I never have forgotten you or the rose! I stole it from the Wainwright's yard after I got done licking Chuck, and I had a fight with Hal Wainwright over it which almost finished the rose, and nearly got me expelled from school before I got through with it. Hal told his mother and she took it to the school board. I was a pretty tough little rascal in those days I guess and no doubt needed some lickings myself occasionally. But I remember I almost lost my nerve when I got back to school that day and came within an ace of stuffing the rose in my pocket instead of throwing it on your desk. I never dreamed the rose would be anything to you. It was only my way of paying tribute to you. You seemed to me something like a rose yourself, just dropped down out of heaven you know, you were so little and pink and gold with such great blue eyes. Pardon me. I don't mean to be too personal. You don't mind a big hobbledehoy's admiration, do you? You were only a baby; but I would have licked any boy in town that lifted a word or a finger against you. And to think you really needed my help! It certainly would have lifted me above the clouds to have known it then!

And now about this war business. Of course it is a rough job, and somebody had to do it for the world. I was glad and willing to do my part; but it makes a different thing out of it to be called a knight, and I guess I'll look at it a little more respectfully now. If a life like mine can protect a life like yours from some of the things those Germans are putting over I'll gladly give it. I've sized it up that a man couldn't do a bigger thing for the world anyhow he planned it than to make the world safe for a life like yours; so me for what they call "the supreme sacrifice," and it won't be any sacrifice at all if it helps you!

No, I haven't got a sweater or those other things that go with those that you talk about. Mother hasn't time to knit and I never was much of a lady's man, I guess you know if you know me at all. Or perhaps you don't. But anyhow I'd be wonderfully pleased to wear a sweater that you knit, although it seems a pretty big thing for you to do for me. However, if knitting is your job in this war, and I wouldn't be robbing any other better fellow, I certainly would just love to have it.

If you could see this big dusty monotonous olive-drab camp you would know what a bright spot your letter and the thought of a real friend has made in it. I suppose you have been thinking all this time that I was neglectful because I didn't answer, but it was all the fault of someone who gave you the wrong address. I am hoping you will forgive me for the delay and that some day you will have time to write to me again.

> Sincerely and proudly,
> Your knight,
> John Cameron

As he walked back to his barracks in the starlight his heart was filled with a great peace. What a thing it was to have been able to speak to her on paper and let her know his thoughts of her. It was as if after all these years he had been able to pluck another trifling rose and lay it at her lovely feet. Her knight! It was the fulfillment of all his boyish dreams!

He had entrusted his letter to the Y.M.C.A. man to mail as he was going out of camp that night and would mail it in Baltimore, ensuring it an immediate start. Now he began to speculate whether it would reach its destination by morning and be delivered with the morning mail. He felt as excited and impatient as a child over it.

Suddenly a voice above him in a barracks window rang out with a familiar guffaw, and the words:

"Why, man, I can't! Didn't I tell you I'm going to marry Ruth Macdonald before I go! There wouldn't be time for that and the other, too!"

Something in his heart grew cold with pain and horror, and something in his motive power stopped suddenly and halted his feet on the sidewalk in the grade cut below the officers' barracks.

"Aw! A week more won't make any difference," drawled another familiar voice, "I say, Hal, she's just crazy about you and you could get no end of information out of her if you tried. All she asks is that you tell what you know about a few little things that don't matter anyway."

"But I tell you I can't, man. If Ruth found out about the girl the mischief would be to pay. She wouldn't stand for another girl—not that kind of a girl, you know, and there wouldn't be time for me to explain and smooth things over before I go across the Pond. I tell you I've made up my mind about this."

The barracks door slammed shut on the voices and Corporal Cameron's heart gave a great jump upwards in his breast and went on. Slowly, dizzily he came to his senses and moved on automatically toward his own quarters.

7

HE had passed the quarters of the signal corps before the thought of the letter he had just written came to his mind. Then he stopped short, gave one agonizing glance toward his barracks only a few feet away, realized that it was nearly time for bed call and that he could not possibly make it if he went back, then whirled about and started out on a wild run like a madman over the ground he had just traveled. He was not conscious of carrying on a train of thought as he ran, his only idea was to get to the Y.M.C.A. hut before the man had left with the letter. Never should his childhood's enemy have that letter to sneer over!

All the pleasant phrases which had flowed from his pen so easily but a few moments before seemed to flare now in letters of fire before his blood-shot eyes as he bounded over the ground. To think he should have lowered himself and weakened his position so, as to write to the girl who was soon to be the wife of that contemptible puppy!

The bugles began to sound taps here and there in the barracks as he flew past, but they meant nothing to him.

Breathless he arrived at the Y.M.C.A. hut just as the last light was being put out. A dark figure stood on the steps as he halted entirely winded, and tried to gasp out: "Where is Mr. Hathaway?" to the assistant who was locking up.

"Oh, he left five minutes after you did," said the man with a yawn. "The rector came by in his car and took him along. Say, you'll be late getting in, Corporal, taps sounded almost five minutes ago."

With a low exclamation of disgust and dismay Cameron turned and started back again in a long swinging stride, his face flushing hotly in the dark over his double predicament. He had gone back for nothing and got himself subject to a calling down, a thing which he had avoided scrupulously since coming to camp, but he was so miserable over the other matter that it seemed a thing of no moment to him now. He was altogether occupied with metaphorically kicking himself for having answered that letter; for having mailed it so soon without ever stopping to read it over or give himself a chance to reconsider. He might have known, he might have remembered that Ruth Macdonald was no comrade for him; that she was a neighbor of the Wainwright's and would in all probability be a friend of the lieutenant's. Not for all that he owned in the world or hoped to own, would he have thus laid himself open to the possibility of having Wainwright know any of his inner thoughts. He would rather have lived and died unknown, unfriended, than that this should come to pass.

And she? The promised wife of Wainwright! Could it be? She must have written him that letter merely from a fine friendly patronage. All right, of course, from her standpoint, but from his, gall and wormwood to his proud spirit. Oh, that he had not answered it! He might have known! He should have remembered that she had never been in his class. Not that his people were not as good as hers, and maybe better, so far as intellectual attainments were concerned; but his had lost their money, had lived a quiet life, and in her eyes and the eyes of her family were very likely as the mere dust of the earth. And now, just now when war had set its seal of sacrifice upon all young men in uniform, he as a soldier had risen to a kind of deified class set apart for hero worship, nothing more. It was not her fault that she had been brought up that way, and that he seemed so to her, and nothing more. She had shown her beautiful spirit in giving him the tribute that seemed worthiest to her view. He would not blame her, nor despise her, but he would hold himself aloof as he had done in the past, and show her that he wanted no favors, no patronage. He was sufficient to himself. What galled him most was to think that perhaps in the intimacy of their engagement she might show his letter to Wainwright, and they would laugh together over him, a poor soldier, presuming to write as he had done to a girl in her station. They would laugh together, half pitifully—at least the woman would be pitiful, the man was likely to sneer. He could see his hateful mustache curl now with scorn and his little eyes twinkle. And he would tell her all the lies he had tried to put upon him in the past. He would give her a wrong idea of his character. He would rejoice and triumph to do so! Oh, the bitterness of it! It overwhelmed him so that the little matter of getting into his bunk without being seen by the officer in charge was utterly over-looked by him.

Perhaps some good angel arranged the way for him so that he was able to slip past the guards without being challenged. Two of the guards were talking at the corner of the barracks with their backs to him at the particular second when he came in sight. A minute later they turned back to their monotonous march and the shadow of the vanishing corporal had just disappeared from among the other dark shadows of the night landscape. Inside the barracks another guard welcomed him eagerly without questioning his presence there at that hour:

"Say, Cam, how about day after to-morrow? Are you free? Will you take my place on guard? I want to go up to Philadelphia and see my girl, and I'm sure of a pass, but I'm listed for guard duty. I'll do the same for you sometime."

"Sure!" said Cameron heartily, and swung up stairs with a sudden realization that he had been granted a streak of good luck. Yet somehow he did not seem to care much.

He tiptoed over to his bunk among the rows of sleeping forms, removed from it a pair of shoes, three books, some newspapers and a mess kit which some lazy comrades had left there, and threw himself down with scant undressing. It seemed as though a great calamity had befallen him, although when he tried to reason it out he could not understand how things were so much changed from what they had been that morning before he received the letter. Ruth Macdonald had never been anything in his life but a lovely picture. There was no slightest possibility that she would ever be more. She was like a distant star to be admired but never come near. Had he been fool enough to have his head turned by her writing that kind letter to him? Had he even remotely fancied she would ever be anything nearer to him than just a formal friend who occasionally stooped to give a bright smile or do a kindness? Well, if he had, he needed this knock-down blow. It might be a good thing that it came so soon before he had let this thing grow in his imagination; but oh, if it had but come a bit sooner! If it had only been on the way over to the Y.M.C.A. hut instead of on the way back that letter would never have been written! She would have set him down as a boor perhaps, but what matter? What was she to him, or he to her? Well—perhaps he would have written a letter briefly to thank her for her offer of knitting, but it would have been an entirely different letter from the one he did write. He ground his teeth as he thought out the letter he should have written:

> My Dear Miss Macdonald: (No "friend" about that.)
>
> It certainly was kind of you to think of me as a possible recipient of a sweater. But I feel that there are other boys who perhaps need things more than I do. I am well supplied with all necessities. I appreciate your interest in an old school friend. The life of a soldier is not so bad, and I imagine we shall have no end of novel experiences before the war is over. I hope we shall be able to put an end to this terrible struggle very soon when we get over and make the world a safe and happy place for you and your friends. Here's hoping the men who are your special friends will all come home safe and sound and soon.
>
> > Sincerely,
> > J. Cameron

He wrote that letter over and over mentally as he tossed on his bunk in the dark, changing phrases and whole sentences. Perhaps it would be better to say something about "her officer friends" and make it very clear to her that he understood his own distant position with her. Then suddenly he kicked the big blue blanket off and sat up with a deep sigh. What a fool he was. He could not write another letter. The letter was gone, and as it was written he must abide by it. He could not get it back or unwrite it much as he wished it. There was no excuse, or way to make it possible to write and refuse those sweaters and things, was there?

He sat staring into the darkness while the man in the next bunk roused to toss back his blanket which had fallen superfluously across his face, and to mutter some sleepy imprecations. But Cameron was off on the composition of another letter:

> My Dear Miss Macdonald:
> I have been thinking it over and have decided that I do not need a sweater or any of those other things you mention. I really am pretty well supplied with necessities, and you know they don't give us much room to put anything around the barracks. There must be a lot of other fellows who need them more, so I will decline that you may give your work to others who have nothing, or to those who are your personal friends.
> Very truly,
> J. Cameron

Having convinced his turbulent brain that it was quite possible for him to write such a letter as this, he flung himself miserably back on his hard cot again and realized that he did not want to write it. That it would be almost an insult to the girl, who even if she had been patronizing him, had done it with a kind intent, and after all it was not her fault that he was a fool. She had a right to marry whom she would. Certainly he never expected her to marry him. Only he had to own to himself that he wanted those things she had offered. He wanted to touch something she had worked upon, and feel that it belonged to him. He wanted to keep this much of human friendship for himself. Even if she was going to marry another man, she had always been his ideal of a beautiful, lovable woman, and as such she should stay his, even if she married a dozen enemy officers!

It was then he began to see that the thing that was really making him miserable was that she was giving her sweet young life to such a rotten little mean-natured man as Wainwright. That was the real pain. If some fine noble man like—well—like Captain La Rue, only younger, of course, should come along he would be glad for her. But this excuse for a man! Oh, it was outrageous! How could she be so deceived? and yet, of course, women knew very little of men. They had no standards by which to judge them. They had no opportunity to see them except in plain sight of those they wished to please. One could not expect them to have discernment in selecting their friends. But what a pity! Things were all wrong! There ought to be some way to educate a woman so that she would realize the dangers all about her and be somewhat protected. It was worse for Ruth Macdonald because she had no men in her family who could protect her. Her old grandfather was the only near living male relative and he was a hopeless invalid, almost entirely confined to the house. What could he know of the young men who came to court his granddaughter? What did he remember of the ways of men, having been so many years shut away from their haunts?

The corporal tossed on his hard cot and sighed like a furnace. There ought to be some one to protect her. Someone ought to make her understand what kind of a fellow Wainwright was! She had called him her knight, and a knight's business was to protect, yet what could he do? He could not go to her and tell her that the man she was going to marry was rotten and utterly without moral principle. He could not even send some one else to warn her. Who could he send? His mother? No, his mother would feel shy and afraid of a girl like that. She had always lived a quiet life. He doubted if she would understand herself how utterly unfit a mate Wainwright was for a good pure girl. And there was no one else in the world that he could send. Besides, if she loved the man, and incomprehensible as it seemed, she must love him or why should she marry him?—if she loved him she would not believe an angel from heaven against him. Women were that way; that is, if they were good women, like Ruth. Oh, to think of her tied up to that—*beast!* He could think of no other word. In his agony he rolled on his face and groaned aloud.

"Oh God!" his soul cried out, "why do such things have to be? If there really is a God why does He let such awful things happen to a pure good girl? The same old bitter question that had troubled the hard young days of his own life. Could there be a God who cared when bitterness was in so many cups? Why had God let the war come?"

Sometime in the night the tumult in his brain and heart subsided and he fell into a profound sleep. The next thing he knew the kindly roughness of his comrades wakened him with shakes and wet sponges flying through the air, and he opened his consciousness to the world again and heard the bugle blowing for roll call. Another day had dawned grayly and he must get up. They set him on his feet, and bantered him into action, and he responded with his usual wit that put them all in howls of laughter, but as he stumbled into place in the line in the five o'clock dawning he realized that a heavy weight was on his heart which he tried to throw off. What did it matter what Ruth Macdonald did with her life? She was nothing to him, never had been and never could be. If only he had not written that letter all would now be as it always had been. If only she had not written her letter! Or no! He put his hand to his breast pocket with a quick movement of protection. Somehow he was not yet ready to relinquish that one taste of bright girl friendliness, even though it had brought a stab in its wake.

He was glad when the orders came for him and five other fellows to tramp across the camp to the gas school and go through two solid hours of instruction ending with a practical illustration of the gas mask and a good dose of gas. It helped to put his mind on the great business of war which was to be his only business now until it or he were ended. He set his lips grimly and went about his work vigorously. What did it matter, anyway, what she thought of him? He need never answer another letter, even if she wrote. He need not accept the package from the post office. He could let them send it back— refuse it and let them send it back, that was what he could do! Then she might think what she liked. Perhaps she would suppose him already gone to France. Anyhow, he would forget her! It was the only sensible thing to do.

Meanwhile the letter had flown on its way with more than ordinary swiftness, as if it had known that a force was seeking to bring it back again. The Y.M.C.A. man was carried at high speed in an automobile to the nearest station to the camp, and arrived in time to catch the Baltimore train just stopping. In the Baltimore station he went to mail the letter just as the letter gatherer arrived with his keys to open the box. So the letter lost no time but was sorted and started northward before midnight, and by some happy chance arrived at its destination in time to be laid by Ruth Macdonald's plate at lunch time the next day.

Some quick sense must have warned Ruth, for she

gathered her mail up and slipped it unobtrusively into the pocket of her skirt before it could be noticed. Dottie Wetherill had come home with her for lunch and the bright red Y.M.C.A. triangle on the envelope was so conspicuous. Dottie was crazy over soldiers and all things military. She would be sure to exclaim and ask questions. She was one of those people who always found out everything about you that you did not keep under absolute lock and key.

Every day since she had written her letter to Cameron Ruth had watched for an answer, her cheeks glowing sometimes with the least bit of mortification that she should have written at all to have received this rebuff. Had he, after all, misunderstood her? Or had the letter gone astray, or the man gone to the front? She had almost given up expecting an answer now after so many weeks, and the nice warm olive-drab sweater and neatly knitted socks with extra long legs and bright lines of color at the top, with the wristlets and muffler lay wrapped in tissue paper at the very bottom of a drawer in the chiffonier where she would seldom see it and where no one else would ever find it and question her. Probably by and by when the colored draftees were sent away she would get them out and carry them down to the headquarters to be given to some needy man. She felt humiliated and was beginning to tell herself that it was all her own fault and a good lesson for her. She had even decided not to go and see John Cameron's mother again lest that, too, might be misunderstood. It seemed that the frank true instincts of her own heart had been wrong, and she was getting what she justly deserved for departing from Aunt Rhoda's strictly conventional code.

Nevertheless, the letter in her pocket which she had not been able to look at carefully enough to be sure if she knew the writing, crackled and rustled and set her heart beating excitedly, and her mind to wondering what it might be. She answered Dottie Wetherill's chatter with distraught monosyllables and absent smiles, hoping that Dottie would feel it necessary to go home soon after lunch.

But it presently became plain that Dottie had no intention of going home soon; that she had come for a purpose and that she was plying all her arts to accomplish it. Ruth presently roused from her reverie to realize this and set herself to give Dottie as little satisfaction as possible out of her task. It was evident that she had been sent to discover the exact standing and relation in which Ruth held Lieutenant Harry Wainwright. Ruth strongly suspected that Dottie's brother Bob had been the instigator of the mission, and she had no intention of giving him the information.

So Ruth's smiles came out and the inscrutable twinkle grew in her lovely eyes. Dottie chattered on sentence after sentence, paragraph after paragraph, theme after them, always rounding up at the end with some perfectly obvious leading question. Ruth answered in all apparent innocence and sincerity, yet with an utterly different turn of the conversation from what had been expected, and with an indifference that was hopelessly baffling unless the young ambassador asked a point blank question, which she hardly dared to do of Ruth Macdonald without more encouragement. And so at last a long two hours dragged thus away, and finally Dottie Wetherill at the end of her small string, and at a loss for more themes on which to trot around again to the main idea, reluctantly accepted her defeat and took herself away, leaving Ruth to her long delayed letter.

8

RUTH sat looking into space with starry eyes and glowing cheeks after she had read the letter. It seemed to her a wonderful letter, quite the most wonderful she had ever received. Perhaps it was because it fitted so perfectly with her ideal of the writer, who from her little girlhood had always been a picture of what a hero must be. She used to dream big things about him when she was a child. He had been the best baseball player in school when he was ten, and the handsomest little rowdy in town, as well as the boldest, bravest champion of the little girls.

As she grew older and met him occasionally she had always been glad that he kept his old hero look though often appearing in rough garb. She had known they were poor. There had been some story about a loss of money and a long expensive sickness of the father's following an accident which made all the circumstances most trying, but she had never heard the details. She only knew that most of the girls in her set looked on him as a nobody and would no more have companied with him than with their father's chauffeur. After he grew older and began to go to college some of the girls began to think he was good looking, and to say it was quite commendable in him to try to get an education. Some even unearthed the fact that his had been a fine old family in former days and that there had been wealth and servants once. But the story died down as John Cameron walked his quiet way apart, keeping to his old friends, and not responding to the feeble advances of the girls. Ruth had been away at school in these days and had seldom seen him. When she had there had always been that lingering admiration for him from the old days. She had told herself that of course he could not be worth much or people would know him. He was probably ignorant and uncultured, and a closer acquaintance would show him far from what her young ideas had pictured her hero. But somehow that day at the station, the look in his face had revealed fine feeling, and she was glad now to have her intuition concerning him verified by his letter.

And what a letter it was! Why, no young man of her acquaintance could have written with such poetic delicacy. That paragraph about the rose was beautiful, and not a bit too presuming, either, in one who had been a perfect stranger all these years. She liked his simple frankness and the easy way he went back twelve years and began just where they left off. There was none of the bold forwardness that might have been expected in one who had not moved in cultured society. There was no unpleasant assumption of familiarity which might have emphasized her fear that she had overstepped the bounds of convention in writing to him in the first place. On the contrary, her humiliation at his long delayed answer was all forgotten now. He had understood her perfectly and accepted her letter in exactly the way she had meant it without the least bit of foolishness or unpleasantness. In short, he had written the sort of a letter that the kind of man she had always thought—hoped—he was would be likely to write, and it gave her a surprisingly pleasant feeling of satisfaction. It was as if she had discovered a friend all of her own not made for her by her family, nor one to whom she fell heir because of her wealth and position; but just one she had found, out in the great world of souls.

If he had been going to remain at home there might have been a number of questions, social and conventional, which would have arisen to bar the way to this free feeling of a friendship, and which she would have had to meet and reason with before her mind would have shaken itself unhampered; but because he was going away and on such an errand, perhaps never to return, the matter of what her friends might think or what the world would say, simply did not enter into the question at all. The war had lifted them both above such ephemeral barriers into the place of vision where a soul was a soul no matter what he possessed or who he was. So, as she sat in her big white room with all its dainty accessories to a luxurious life, fit setting for a girl so lovely, she smiled unhindered at this bit of beautiful friendship that had suddenly drifted down at her feet out of a great outside unknown world. She touched the letter thoughtfully with caressing fingers, and the kind of a high look in her eyes that a lady of old must have worn when she thought of her knight. It came to her to wonder that she had not felt so about any other of her men friends who had gone into the service. Why should this special one soldier boy represent the whole war, as it were, in this way to her. However, it was but a passing thought, and with a smile still upon her lips she went to the drawer and brought out the finely knitted garments she had made, wrapping them up with care and sending them at once upon their way. It somehow gave her pleasure to set aside a small engagement she had for that afternoon until she had posted the package herself.

Even then, when she took her belated way to a little gathering in honor of one of her girl friends who was going to be married the next week to a young aviator, she kept the smile on her lips and the dreamy look in her eyes, and now and then brought herself back from the chatter around her to remember that something pleasant had happened. Not that there was any foolishness in her thoughts. There was too much dignity and simplicity about the girl, young as she was, to allow her to deal even with her own thoughts in any but a maidenly way, and it was not in the ordinary way of a maid with a man that she thought of this young soldier. He was so far removed from her life in every way, and all the well-drilled formalities, that it never occurred to her to think of him in the same way she thought of her other men friends.

A friend who understood her, and whom she could understand. That was what she had always wanted and what she had never quite had with any of her young associates. One or two had approached to that, but always there had been a point at which they had fallen short. That she should make this man her friend whose letter crackled in her pocket, in that intimate sense of the word, did not occur to her even now. He was somehow set apart for service in her mind; and as such she had chosen him to be her special knight, she to be the lady to whom he might look for encouragement—whose honor he was going forth to defend. It was a misty dreamy ideal of a thought. Somehow she would not have picked out any other of her boy friends to be a knight for her. They were too flippant, too careless and light hearted. The very way in which they lighted their

multitudinous cigarettes and flipped the match away
gave impression that they were going to have the time
of their lives in this war. They might have patriotism
down at the bottom of all this froth and boasting,
doubtless they had; but there was so little seriousness
about them that one would never think of them as
knights, defenders of some great cause of righteousness.
Perhaps she was all wrong. Perhaps it was only her old
baby fancy for the little boy who could always "lick" the
other boys and save the girls from trouble that prejudiced
her in his favor, but at least it was pleasant and a great
relief to know that her impulsive letter had not been
misunderstood.

The girls prattled of this one and that who were
"going over" soon, told of engagements and marriages
soon to occur; criticized the brides and grooms to be;
declared their undying opinions about what was fitting
for a war bride to wear; and whether they would like to
marry a man who had to go right into war and might
return minus an arm or an eye. They discoursed about
the U-boats with a frothy cheerfulness that made Ruth
shudder; and in the same breath told what nice eyes a
young captain had who had recently visited the town,
and what perfectly lovely uniforms he wore. They ar-
gued with serious zeal whether a girl should wear an
olive-drab suit this year if she wanted to look really
smart.

They were the girls among whom she had been
brought up, and Ruth was used to their froth, but
somehow to-day it bored her beyond expression. She
was glad to make an excuse to get away and she drove
her little car around by the way of John Cameron's home
hoping perhaps to get a glimpse of his mother again. But
the house had a shut up look behind the vine that he had
trained, as if it were lonely and lying back in a long wait

till he should come—or not come! A pang went through her heart. For the first time she thought what it meant for a young life like that to be silenced by cold steel. The home empty! The mother alone! His ambitions and hopes unfulfilled! It came to her, too, that if he were her knight he might have to die for her—for his cause! She shuddered and swept the unpleasant thought away, but it had left its mark and would return again.

On the way back she passed a number of young soldiers home on twenty-four hour leave from the nearby camps. They saluted most eagerly, and she knew that any one of them would have gladly occupied the vacant seat in her car, but she was not in the mood to talk with them. She felt that there was something to be thought out and fixed in her mind, some impression that life had for her that afternoon that she did not want to lose in the mild fritter of gay banter that would be sure to follow if she stopped and took home some of the boys. So she bowed graciously and swept by at a high speed as if in a great hurry. The war! The war! It was beating itself into her brain again in much the same way it had done on that morning when the drafted men went away, only now it had taken on a more personal touch. She kept seeing the lonely vine-clad house where that one soldier had lived, and which he had left so desolate. She kept thinking how many such homes and mothers there must be in the land.

That evening when she was free to go to her room she read John Cameron's letter again, and then, feeling almost as if she were childish in her haste, she sat down and wrote an answer. Somehow that second reading made her feel his wish for an answer. It seemed a mute appeal that she could not resist.

When John Cameron received that letter and the accompanying package he was lifted into the seventh heaven for a little while. He forgot all his misgivings, he even forgot Lieutenant Wainwright who had but that day become a most formidable foe, having been transferred to Cameron's company, where he was liable to be commanding officer in absence of the captain, and where frequent salutes would be inevitable. It had been a terrible blow to Cameron. But now it suddenly seemed a small matter. He put on his new sweater and swelled around the way the other boys did, letting them all admire him. He examined the wonderful socks almost reverently, putting a large curious finger gently on the red and blue stripes and thrilling with the thought that her fingers had plied the needles in those many, many stitches to make them. He almost felt it would be sacrilege to wear them, and he laid them away most carefully and locked them into the box under his bed lest some other fellow should admire and desire them to his loss. But with the letter he walked away into the woods as far as the bounds of the camp would allow and read and re-read it, rising at last from it as one refreshed from a comforting meal after long fasting. It was on the way back to his barracks that night, walking slowly under the starlight, not desiring to be back until the last minute before night taps because he did not wish to break the wonderful evening he had spent with her, that he resolved to try to get leave the next Saturday and go home to thank her.

Back in the barracks with the others he fairly scintillated with wit and kept his comrades in roars of laughter until the officer of the night suppressed them summarily. But long after the others were asleep he lay thinking of her, and listening to the singing of his soul as he watched a star that twinkled with a friendly gleam through a crack in the room above his cot. Once again there came the thought of God, and a feeling of gratitude for this lovely friendship in his life. If he knew where God was he would like to thank Him. Lying so and looking up to the star he breathed from his heart a wordless thanksgiving.

The next night he wrote and told her he was coming, and asked permission to call and thank her face to face. Then he fairly haunted the post office at mail time the rest of the week hoping for an answer. He had not written his mother about his coming, for he meant not to go this week if there came no word from Ruth. Besides, it would be nice to surprise his mother. Then there was some doubt about his getting a pass anyway, and so between the two anxieties he was kept busy up to the last minute. But Friday evening he got his pass, and in the last mail came a special delivery from Ruth, just a brief note saying she had been away from home when his letter arrived, but she would be delighted to see him on Sunday afternoon as he had suggested.

He felt like a boy let loose from school as he brushed up his uniform and polished his big army shoes while his less fortunate companions kidded him about the girl he was going to see. He denied their thrusts joyously, in his heart repudiating any such personalities, yet somehow it was pleasant. He had never realized how pleasant it would be to have a girl and be going to see her—such a girl! Of course, she was not for him—not with that possessiveness. But she was a friend, a real friend, and he would not let anything spoil the pleasure of that!

He had not thought anything in his army experience could be so exciting as that first ride back home again. Somehow the deference paid to his uniform got into his blood and made him feel that people all along the line really did care for what the boys were doing for them. It made camp life and hardships seem less dreary.

It was great to get back to his little mother and put his big arms around her again. She seemed so small. Had she shrunken since he left her or was he grown so much huskier with the out of door life? Both, perhaps, and he looked at her sorrowfully. She was so little and quiet and brave to bear life all alone. If he only could get back and get to succeeding in life so that he might make some brightness for her. She had borne so much, and she ought not to have looked so old and worn at her age! For a brief instant again his heart was almost bitter, and he wondered what God meant by giving his good little mother so much trouble. Was there a God when such things could be? He resolved to do something about finding out this very day.

It was pleasant to help his mother about the kitchen, saving her as she had not been saved since he left, telling her about the camp, and listening to her tearful admiration of him. She could scarcely take her eyes from him, he seemed so tall and big and handsome in his uniform; he appeared so much older and more manly that her heart yearned for her boy who seemed to be slipping away from her. It was so heavenly blessed to sit down beside him and sew on a button and mend a torn spot in his flannel shirt and have him pat her shoulder now and then contentedly.

Then with pride she sent him down to the store for something nice for dinner, and watched him through the window with a smile, the tears running down her cheeks. How tall and straight he walked! How like his father when she first knew him! She hoped the neighbors all were looking out and would see him. Her boy! Her soldier boy! And he must go away from her, perhaps to die!

But—*he was here to-day!* She would not think of the rest. She would rejoice now in his presence.

He walked briskly down the street past the houses that had been familiar all his life, meeting people who had never been wont to notice him before; and they smiled upon him from afar now; greeted him with enthusiasm, and turned to look after him as he passed on. It gave him a curious feeling to have so much attention from people who had never known him before. It made him feel strangely small, yet filled with a great pride and patriotism for the country that was his, and the government which he now represented to them all. He was something more to them now than just one of the boys about town who had grown up among them. He was a soldier of the United States. He had given his life for the cause of righteousness. The bitterness he might have felt at their former ignoring of him, was all swallowed up in their genuine and hearty friendliness.

He met the white-haired minister, kindly and dignified, who paused to ask him how he liked camp life and to commend him as a soldier; and looking in his strong gentle face John Cameron remembered his resolve.

He flashed a keen look at the gracious countenance and made up his mind to speak:

"I'd like to ask you a question, Doctor Thurlow. It's been bothering me quite a little ever since this matter of going away to fight has been in my mind. Is there any way that a man—that *I* can find God? That is, if there is a God. I've never thought much about it before, but life down there in camp makes a lot of things seem different, and I've been wondering. I'm not sure what I believe. Is there anyway I can found out?"

A pleasant gleam of surprise and delight thrilled into the deep blue eyes of the minister. It was startling. It almost embarrassed him for a moment, it was so unexpected to have a soldier ask a question about God. It was almost mortifying that he had never thought it worth while to take the initiative on that question with the young man.

"Why, certainly!" he said heartily. "Of course, of course. I'm very glad to know you are interested in those things. Couldn't you come in to my study and talk with me. I think I could help you. I'm sure I could."

"I haven't much time," said Cameron shyly, half ashamed now that he had opened his heart to an almost stranger. He was not even his mother's minister, and he was a comparative newcomer in the town. How had he come to speak to him so impulsively?

"I understand, exactly, of course," said the minister with growing eagerness. "Could you come in now for five or ten minutes? I'll turn back with you and you can stop on your way, or we can talk as we go. Were you thinking of uniting with the church? We have our communion the first Sunday of next month. I should be very glad if you could arrange. We have a number of young people coming in now. I'd like to see you come with them. The church is a good safe place to be. It was established by God. It is a school in which to learn of Him. It is—"

"But I'm not what you would call a Christian!" protested Cameron. "I don't even know that I believe in the Bible. I don't know what your church believes. I don't have a very definite idea what any church believes. I would be a hypocrite to stand up and join a church when I wasn't sure there was a God."

"My dear young fellow!" said the minister affectionately. "Not at all! Not at all! The church is the place for young people to come when they have doubts. It is a shelter, and a growing place. Just trust yourself to God and come in among His people and your doubts will vanish. Don't worry about doubts. Many people have doubts. Just let them alone and put yourself in the right way and you will forget them. I should be glad to talk with you further. I would like to see you come into communion with God's people. If you want to find God you should come where He has promised to be. It is a great thing to have a fine young fellow like you, and a soldier, array himself on the side of God. I would like to see you stand up on the right side before you go out to meet danger and perhaps death."

John Cameron stood watching him as he talked.

"He's a good old guy," he thought gravely, "but he doesn't get my point. He evidently believes what he says, but I don't just see going blind-folded into a church. However, there's something to what he says about going where God is if I want to find him."

Out loud he merely said:

"I'll think about it, Doctor, and perhaps come in to see you the next time I'm home." Then he excused himself and went on to the store.

As he walked away he said to himself:

"I wonder what Ruth Macdonald would say if I asked her the same question? I wonder if she has thought anything about it? I wonder if I'd ever have the nerve to ask her?"

The next morning he suggested to his mother that they go to Doctor Thurlow's church together. She would have very much preferred going to her own church with him, but she knew that he did not care for the minister and had never been very friendly with the people, so she put aside her secret wish and went with him. To tell the truth she was very proud to go anywhere with her handsome soldier son, and one thing that made her the more willing was that she remembered that the Macdonalds always went to the Presbyterian church, and perhaps they would be there to-day and Ruth would see them. But she said not a word of this to her boy.

John spent most of the time with his mother. He went up to college for an hour or so Saturday evening, dropping in on his fraternity for a few minutes and realizing what true friends he had among the fellows who were left, though most of them were gone. He walked about the familiar rooms, looking at the new pictures, photographs of his friends in uniform. This one was a lieutenant in Officers' Training Camp. That one had gone with the Ambulance Corps. Tom was with the Engineers, and Jimmie and Sam had joined the Tank Service. Two of the fellows were in France in the front ranks, another had enlisted in the Marines, it seemed that hardly any were left, and of those three had been turned down for some slight physical defect, and were working in munition factories and the ship-yard. Everything was changed. The old playmates had become men with earnest purposes. He did not stay long. There was a restlessness about it all that pulled the strings of his heart, and made him realize how different everything was.

Sunday morning as he walked to church with his mother he wondered why he had never gone more with her when he was at home. It seemed a pleasant thing to do.

The service was beautifully solemn, and Doctor Thurlow had many gracious words to say of the boys in the army, and spent much time reading letters from those at the front who belonged to the church and Sunday school, and spoke of the "supreme sacrifice" in the light of a saving grace; but the sermon was a gentle ponderous thing that got nowhere, spiced toward its close with thrilling scenes from battle news. John Cameron as he listened did not feel that he had found God. He did not feel a bit enlightened by it. He laid it to his own ignorance and stupidity, though, and determined not to give up the search. The prayer at the close of the sermon somehow clinched this resolve because there was something so genuine and sweet and earnest about it. He could not help thinking that the man might know more of God than he was able to make plain to his hearers. He had really never noticed either a prayer or a sermon before in his life. He had sat in the room with very few. He wondered if all sermons and prayers were like these and wished he had noticed them. He had never been much of a church goer.

But the climax, the real heart of his whole two days, was after Sunday dinner when he went out to call upon Ruth Macdonald. And it was characteristic of his whole reticent nature, and the way he had been brought up, that he did not tell his mother where he was going. It had never occurred to him to tell her his movements when they did not directly concern her, and she had never brought herself up to ask him. It is the habit of some women, and many mothers.

A great embarrassment fell upon him as he entered the grounds of the Macdonald place, and when he stood before the plate-glass doors waiting for an answer to his ring he would have turned and fled if he had not promised to come.

It was perhaps not an accident that Ruth let him in herself and took him to a big quiet library with wide-open windows overlooking the lawn, and heavy curtains shutting them in from the rest of the house, where, to his great amazement, he could feel at once at ease with her and talk to her just as he had done in her letters and his own.

Somehow it was like having a lifetime dream suddenly fulfilled to be sitting this way in pleasant converse with her, watching the lights and shadows of expression flit across her sensitive face, and knowing that the light in her eyes was for him. It seemed incredible, but she evidently enjoyed talking to him. Afterwards he thought about it as if their souls had been calling to one another across infinite space, things that neither of them could quite hear, and now they were within hailing distance.

He had thanked her for the sweater and other things, and they had talked a little about the old school days and how life changed people, when he happened to glance out of the window near him and saw a man in officer's uniform approaching. He stopped short in the midst of a sentence and rose, his face set, his eyes still on the rapidly approaching soldiers:

"I'm sorry," he said, "I shall have to go. It's been wonderful to come, but I must go at once. Perhaps you'll let me go out this way. It is a shorter cut. Thank you for everything, and perhaps if there's ever another time—I'd like to come again—"

"Oh, please don't go yet!" she said putting out her hand in protest. But he grasped the hand with a quick impulsive grip and with a hasty: "I'm sorry, but I must!" he opened the glass door to the side piazza and was gone.

In much bewilderment and distress Ruth watched him stride away toward the hedge and disappear. Then she turned to the front window and caught a glimpse of Lieutenant Wainwright just mounting the front steps. What did it all mean?

9

RUTH tried to control her perturbation and meet her guest with an unruffled countenance, but there was something about the bland smug countenance of Lieutenant Wainwright that irritated her. To have her first pleasant visit with Cameron suddenly broken up in this mysterious fashion, and Wainwright substituted for Cameron was somehow like taking a bite of some pleasant fruit and having it turn out plain potato in one's mouth. It was so sudden, like that. She could not seem to get her equilibrium. Her mind was in a whirl of question and she could not focus it on her present caller nor think of anything suitable to say to him. She was not even sure but that he was noticing that she was distraught.

To have John Cameron leave in that precipitate manner at the sight of Harry Wainwright! It was all too evident that he had seen him through the window. But they were fellow townsmen, and had gone to school together! Surely he knew him! Of course, Harry was a superior officer, but Cameron would not be the kind of man to mind that. She could not understand it. There had been a look in his face—a set look! There must be something behind it all. Some reason why he did not want to be seen by Wainwright. Surely Cameron had nothing of which to be ashamed! The thought brought a sudden dismay. What did she know about Cameron after all? A look, a smile, a bit of boyish gallantry. He might be anything but fine in his private life, of course, and Harry might be cognizant of the fact. Yet he did not look like that. Even while the thought forced itself into her mind she resented it and resisted it. Then turning to her guest who was giving an elaborate account of how he had saved a woman's life in an automobile accident, she interrupted him:

"Harry, what do you know about John Cameron?" she asked impulsively.

Wainwright's face darkened with an ugly frown.

"More than I want to know," he answered gruffly. "He's rotten! That's all! Why?" He eyed her suspiciously.

There was something in his tone that put her on the defensive at once:

"Oh, I saw him to-day, and I was wondering," she answered evasively.

"It's one of the annoyances of army life that we have to be herded up with all sorts of cattle!" said Wainwright with a disdainful curl of his baby mustache. "But I didn't come here to talk about John Cameron. I came to tell you that I'm going to be married, Ruth. I'm going to be married before I go to France!"

"Delightful!" said Ruth pleasantly. "Do I know the lady?"

"Indeed you do," he said watching her with satisfaction. "You've known for several years that you were the only one for me, and I've come to tell you that I won't stand any more dallying. I mean business now!"

He crossed his fat leather puttees creakily and swelled out, trying to look firm. He had decided that he must impress her with the seriousness of the occasion.

But Ruth only laughed merrily. He had been proposing to her ever since he got out of short trousers, and she had always laughed him out of it. The first time she told him that she was only a kid and he wasn't much more himself, and she didn't want to hear any more such talk. Of late he had grown less troublesome, and she had been inclined to settle down to the old neighborly playmate relation, so she was not greatly disturbed by the turn of the conversation. In fact, she was too much upset and annoyed by the sudden departure of Cameron to realize the determined note in Wainwright's voice.

"I mean it!" he said in an offended tone, flattening his double chin and rolling out his fat lips importantly. "I'm not to be played with any longer."

Ruth's face sobered:

"I certainly never had an idea of playing with you, Harry. I think I've always been quite frank with you."

Wainwright felt that he wasn't getting on quite as well as he had planned. He frowned and sat up:

"Now see here, Ruth! Let's talk this thing over!" he said, drawing the big leather chair in which he was sitting nearer to hers.

But Ruth's glance had wandered out of the window. "Why, there comes Bobbie Wetherill!" she exclaimed eagerly and slipped out of her chair to the door just as one of Wainwright's smooth fat hands reached out to take hold of the arm of her rocker. "I'll open the door for him. Mary is in the kitchen and may not hear the bell right away."

There was nothing for Wainwright to do but make the best of the situation, although he greeted Wetherill with no very good grace, and his large lips pouted out sulkily as he relaxed into his chair again to await the departure of the intruder.

Lieutenant Wetherill was quite overwhelmed with the warmth of the greeting he received from Ruth and settled down to enjoy it while it lasted. With a wicked glance of triumph at his rival he laid himself out to make his account of camp life as entertaining as possible. He produced a gorgeous box of bonbons and arranged himself comfortably for the afternoon, while Wainwright's brow grew darker and his lips pouted out farther and farther under his petted little moustache. It was all a great bore to Ruth just now with her mind full of the annoyance about Cameron. At least she would have preferred to have had her talk with him and found out what he was with her own judgment. But anything was better than a *tête-à-tête* with Wainwright just now; so she ate bonbons and asked questions, and kept the conversation going, ignoring Wainwright's increasing grouch.

It was a great relief, however, when about half-past four the maid appeared at the door:

"A long distance telephone call for you, Miss Ruth."

As Ruth was going up the stairs to her own private 'phone she paused to fasten the tie of her low shoe that had come undone and was threatening to trip her, and she heard Harry Wainwright's voice in an angry snarl:

"What business did you have coming here to-day, you darned chump! You knew what I came for, and you did it on purpose! If you don't get out the minute she gets back I'll put her wise to you and the kind of girls you go with in no time. And you needn't think you can turn the tables on me, either, for I'll fix you so you won't dare open your fool mouth!"

The sentence finished with an oath and Ruth hurried into her room and shut the door with a sick kind of feeling that her whole little world was turning black about her.

It was good to hear the voice of her cousin, Captain La Rue, over the 'phone, even though it was but a message that he could not come as he had promised that evening. It reassured her that there were good men in the world. Of course, he was older, but she was sure he had never been what people called "wild," although he had plenty of courage and spirit. She had often heard that good men were few, but it had never seemed to apply to her world but vaguely. Now here of a sudden a slur had been thrown at three of her young world. John Cameron, it is true, was a comparative stranger, and, of course, she had no means of judging except by the look in his eyes. She understood in a general way that "rotten" as applied to a young man's character implied uncleanness. John Cameron's eyes were steady and clear. They did not look that way. But then, how could she tell? And here, this very minute she had been hearing that Bobbie Wetherill's life was not all that it should be and Wainwright had tacitly accepted the possibility of the same weakness in himself. These were boys with whom she had been brought up. Selfish and conceited she had often thought them on occasion, but it had not occurred to her that there might be anything worse. She pressed her hands to her eyes and tried to force a calm steadiness into her soul. Somehow she had an utter distaste for going back into that library and hearing their boastful chatter. Yet she must go. She had been hoping all the afternoon for her cousin's arrival to send the other two away. Now that was out of the question and she must use her own tact to get pleasantly rid of them. With a sigh she opened her door and started down stairs again.

It was Wainwright's blatant voice again that broke

through the Sabbath afternoon stillness of the house as she approached the library door:

"Yes, I've got John Cameron all right now!" he laughed. "He won't hold his head so high after he's spent a few days in the guard-house. And that's what they're all going to get that are late coming back this time. I found out before I left camp that his pass only reads till eleven o'clock and the five o'clock train is the last one he can leave Chester on to get him to camp by eleven. So I hired a fellow that was coming up to buddy-up to Cam and fix it that he is to get a friend of his to take them over to Chester in time for the train. The fellow don't have to get back himself to-night at all, but he isn't going to let on, you know, so Cam will think they're in the same boat. Then they're going to have a little bit of tire trouble, down in that lonely bit of rough road, that short cut between here and Chester, where there aren't any cars passing to help them out, and they'll miss the train at Chester. See? And then the man will offer to take them on to camp in his car and they'll get stuck again down beyond Wilmington, lose the road, and switch off toward Singleton—you know, where we took those girls to that little out-of-the-way tavern that time—and you see Cam getting back to camp in time, don't you?"

Ruth had paused with her hand on the heavy portiere, wide-eyed.

"But Cameron'll find a way out. He's too sharp. He'll start to walk, or he'll get some passing car to take him," said Wetherill with conviction.

"No, he won't. The fellows are all primed. They're going to catch him in spots where cars don't go, where the road is bad, you know, and nobody but a fool would go with a car. He won't be noticing before they break down because this fellow told him his man could drive a car over the moon and never break down. Besides, I know my men. They'll get away with the job. There's too much money in it for them to run any risk of losing out. It's all going to happen so quick he won't be ready for anything."

"Well, you'll have your trouble for your pains. Cam'll explain everything to the officers and he'll get by. He always does."

"Not this time. They've just made a rule that no excuses go. There've been a lot of fellows coming back late drunk. And you see that's how we mean to wind up. They are going to get him drunk, and then we'll see if little Johnnie will go around with his nose in the air any longer! I'm going to run down to the tavern late this evening to see the fun myself!"

"You can't do it! Cam won't drink! It's been tried again and again. He'd rather die!"

But the girl at the door had fled to her room on velvet shod feet and closed her door, her face white with horror, her lips set with purpose, her heart beating wildly. She must put a stop somehow to this diabolical plot against him. Whether he was worthy or not they should not do this thing to him! She rang for the maid and began putting on her hat and coat and flinging a few things into a small bag. She glanced at her watch. It was a quarter to five. Could she make it? If she only knew which way he had gone! Would his mother have a telephone? Her eyes scanned the C column hurriedly. Yes, there it was. She might have known he would not allow her to be alone without a telephone.

The maid appeared at the door.

"Mary," she said, trying to speak calmly, "tell Thomas to have the gray car ready at once. He needn't bring it to the house, I will come out the back way. Please take this bag and two long coats out, and when I am gone go to the library and ask the two gentlemen there to excuse me. Say that I am suddenly called away to a friend in trouble. If Aunt Rhoda returns soon tell her I will call her up later and let her know my plans. That is all. I will be down in two or three minutes and I wish to start without delay!"

Mary departed on her errand and Ruth went to the telephone and called up the Cameron number.

The sadness of the answering voice struck her even in her haste. Her own tone was eager, intimate, as she hastened to convey her message.

"Mrs. Cameron, this is Ruth Macdonald. Has your son left yet? I was wondering if he would care to be taken to the train in our car?"

"Oh! he has *just gone!*" came a pitiful little gasp that had a sob at the end of it. "He went in somebody's car and they were late coming. I'm afraid he is going to miss his train and he has got to get it or he will be in trouble! That is the last train that connects with Wilmington."

Ruth's heart leaped to her opportunity.

"Suppose we try to catch him then," proposed Ruth gleefully. "My car can go pretty fast, and if he has missed the train perhaps we can carry him on to Wilmington. Would you like to try?"

"Oh, could we?" the voice throbbed with eagerness.

"Hurry up then. My car is all ready. I'll be down there in three minutes. We've no time to waste. Put on something warm!"

She hung up the receiver without waiting for further reply, and hurried softly out of the room and down the back stairs.

Thomas was well trained. The cars were always in order. He was used to Ruth's hurry calls, and when she reached the garage she found the car standing in the back street waiting for her. In a moment more she was rushing on her way toward the village without having aroused the suspicion of the two men who so impatiently awaited her return. Mrs. Cameron was ready, eager as a child, standing on the sidewalk with a great blanket shawl over her arm and looking up the street for her.

It was not until they had swept through the village, over the bridge, and were out on the broad highway toward Chester that Ruth began to realize what a wild goose chase she had undertaken. Just where did she expect to find them, anyway? It was now three minutes to five by the little clock in the car and it was a full fifteen minutes' drive to Chester. The plan had been to delay him on the way to the train, and there had been mention of a short cut. Could that be the rough stony road that turned down sharply just beyond the stone quarry? It seemed hardly possible that anybody would attempt to run a car over that road. Surely John Cameron knew the roads about here well enough to advise against it. Still, Ruth knew the locality like a book and that was the only short cut thereabout. If they had gone down there they might emerge at the other end just in time to miss the train, and then start on toward Wilmington. Or they might turn back and take the longer way if they found the short road utterly impassable. Which should she take? Should she dare that rocky way? If only there might be some tracks to guide her. But the road was hard and dusty and told no tales of recent travelers. They skimmed down the grade past the stone quarry, and the short cut flashed into view, rough and hilly, turning sharply away behind a group of spruce trees. It was thick woods beyond. If she went that way and got into any trouble with her machine the chances were few that anyone would come along to help. She had but a moment to decide, and something told her that the long way was the safe one and shorter in the end. She swept on, her engine throbbing with that pleasant purr of expensive well-groomed machinery, the car leaping forward as if it delighted in the high speed. The little woman by her side sat breathless and eager, with shining eyes, looking ahead for her boy.

They passed car after car, and Ruth scanned the occupants keenly. Some were filled with soldiers, but John Cameron was not among them. She began to be afraid that perhaps she ought after all to have gone down that hilly way and made sure they were not there. She was not quite sure where that short road came out. If she knew she might run up a little way from this further end.

They two women sat almost silent, straining their eyes ahead. They had said hardly a word since the first greeting. Each seemed to understand the thought of the other without words. For the present they had but one common object, to find John Cameron.

Suddenly, as far ahead as they could see, a car darted out of the wooded roadside, swung into their road and plunged ahead at a tremendous rate. They had a glimpse of khaki uniforms, but it was much too far away to distinguish faces or forms. Nevertheless, both women fastened their eyes upon it with but one thought. Ruth put on more speed and forged ahead, thankful that she was not within city lines yet, and that there was no one about to remind her of the speed limit. Something told her that the man she was seeking was in that car ahead.

It was a thrilling race. Ruth said no word, but she knew that her companion was aware that she was chasing that car. Mrs. Cameron sat straight and tense as if it had been a race of life and death, her cheeks glowing and her eyes shining. Ruth was grateful that she did not talk. Some women would have talked incessantly.

The other car did not go into Chester proper at all, but veered away into a branch road and Ruth followed, leaping over the road as if it had been a gray velvet ribbon. She did not seem to be gaining on the car; but it was encouraging that they could keep it still in sight. Then there came a sharp turn of the road and it was gone. They were pulsing along now at a tremendous rate. The girl had cast caution to the winds. She was hearing the complacent sneer of Harry Wainwright as he boasted how they would get John Cameron into trouble, and all the force of her strong young will was enlisted to frustrate his plans.

It was growing dusk, and lights leaped out on the munition factories all about them. Along the river other lights flashed and flickered in the white mist that rose like a wreath. But Ruth saw nothing of it all. She was straining her eyes for the little black speck of a car which she had been following and which now seemed to be swallowed up by the evening. She had not relaxed her speed, and the miles were whirling by, and she had a growing consciousness that she might be passing the object of her chase at any minute without knowing it. Presently they came to a junction of three roads, and she paused. On ahead the road was broad and empty save for a car coming towards them. Off to the right was a desolate way leading to a little cemetery. Down to the left a smooth wooded road wound into the darkness. There were sign boards up. Ruth leaned out and flashed a pocket torch on the board. "To Pine Tree Inn, 7 Miles" it read. Did she fancy it or was it really true that she could hear the distant sound of a car among the pines?

"I'm going down this way!" she said decidedly to her companion, as if her action needed an explanation, and she turned her car into the new road.

"But it's too late now," said Mrs. Cameron wistfully. "The train will be gone, of course, even from Wilmington. And you ought to be going home. I'm very wrong to have let you come so far; and it's getting dark. Your folks will by worrying about you. That man will likely do his best to get him to camp in time."

"No," said Ruth decidedly, "there's no one at home to worry just now, and I often go about alone rather late. Besides, aren't we having a good time? We're going a little further anyway before we give up."

She began to wonder in her heart if she ought not to have told somebody else and taken Thomas along to help. It was rather a questionable thing for her to do, in the dusk of the evening—two women all alone. But then, she had Mrs. Cameron along and that made it perfectly respectable. But if she failed now, what else could she do? Her blood boiled hotly at the thought of letting Harry Wainwright succeed in his miserable plot. Oh, for cousin La Rue! He would have thought a way out of this. If everything else failed she would tell the whole story to Captain La Rue and beg him to exonerate John Cameron. But that, of course, she know would be hard to do, there was so much red tape in the army, and there were so many unwritten laws that could not be set aside just for private individuals. Still, there must be a way if she had to go herself to someone and tell what she had overheard. She set her pretty lips firmly and rode on at a brisk pace down the dark road, switching on her headlights to see the way here in the woods. And then suddenly, just in time she jerked on the brake and came to a jarring stop, for ahead of her a big car was sprawled across the road, and there, rising hurriedly from a kneeling posture before the engine, in the full blaze of her headlights, blinking and frowning with anxiety, stood John Cameron!

10

THE end of her chase came so unexpectedly that her wits were completely scattered. Now that she was face to face with the tall soldier she had nothing to say for her presence there. What would he think of her? How could she explain her coming? She had undertaken the whole thing in such haste that she had not planned ahead. Now she knew that from the start she had understood that she must not explain how she came to be possessed of any information concerning him. She felt a kind of responsible shame for her old playmate Harry Wainwright, and a certain loyalty toward her own social set that prevented her from that, the only possible explanation that could make her coming justifiable. So, now in the brief interval before he had recognized them she must stage the next act, and she found herself unable to speak, her throat dry, her lips for the instant paralyzed. It was the jubilant little mother that stepped into the crisis and did the most natural thing in the world:

"John! Oh John! It's really you! We've caught you!" she cried, and the troubled young soldier peering into the dusk to discover if here was a vehicle he might presume to commandeer to help him out of his predicament lifted startled eyes to the two faces in the car and strode forward, abandoning with a clang the wrench with which he had been working on the car.

"Mother!" he said, a shade of deep anxiety in his voice. "What is the matter? How came you to be here?"

"Why, I came after you," she said laughing like a girl. "We're going to see that you get to camp in time. We've made pretty good time so far. Jump in quick and we'll tell you the rest on the way. We mustn't waste time."

Cameron's startled gaze turned on Ruth now, and a great wonder and delight sprang up in his eyes. It was like the day when he went away on the train, only more so, and it brought a rich flush into Ruth's cheeks. As she felt the hot waves she was glad that she was sitting behind the light.

"What! You?" he breathed wonderingly. "But this is too much! And after the way I treated you!"

His mother looked wonderingly from one to the other:

"Get in, John, quick. We mustn't lose a minute. Something might delay us later." It was plain she was deeply impressed with the necessity for the soldier not to be found wanting.

"Yes, please get in quickly, and let us start. Then we can talk!" said Ruth casting an anxious glance toward the other car.

His hand went out to the door to open it, the wonder still shining in his face, when a low murmur like a growl went up behind him.

Ruth looked up, and there in the full glare of the lights stood two burly civilians and a big soldier:

"Oh, I say!" drawled the soldier in no very pleasant tone, "you're not going to desert us that way! Not after

Pass came out of his way for us! I didn't think you had a yellow streak!"

Cameron paused and a troubled look came into his face. He glanced at the empty back seat with a repression of his disappointment in the necessity.

"There's another fellow here that has to get back at the same time I do," he said looking at Ruth hesitatingly.

"Certainly. Ask him, of course." Ruth's voice was hearty and put the whole car at his disposal.

"There's room for you, too, Chalmers," he said with relief. "And Passmore will be glad to get rid of us I suspect. He'll be able to get home soon. There isn't much the matter with that engine. If you do what I told you to that carburetor you'll find it will go all right. Come on, Chalmers. We ought to hurry!"

"No thanks! I stick to my friends!" said the soldier shortly.

"As you please!" said Cameron stepping on the running board.

"Not as *you* please!" said a gruff voice, "I'm running this party and we all go together? See?" A heavy hand came down upon Cameron's shoulder with a mighty grip.

Cameron landed a smashing blow under the man's chin which sent him reeling and sprang inside as Ruth threw in the clutch and sent her car leaping forward. The two men in front were taken by surprise and barely got out of the way in time, but instantly recovered their senses and sprang after the car, the one nearest her reaching for the wheel. Cameron leaning forward sent him rolling down the gully, and Ruth turned the car sharply to avoid the other car which was occupying as much of the road as possible, and left the third man scrambling to his knees behind her. It was taking a big chance to dash past that car in the narrow space over rough ground, but Ruth was not conscious of anything but the necessity of getting away. In an instant they were back in the road and flashing along through the dark.

"Mother, you better let me help you back here," said her son leaning forward and almost lifting his mother into the back seat, then stepping over to take her place beside Ruth.

"Better turn out your back lights!" he said in a quiet, steady voice. "They might follow, you know. They're in an ugly mood. They've been drinking."

"Then the car isn't really out of commission?"

"Not seriously."

"We're not on the right road, did you know? This road goes to The Pine Tree Inn and Singleton!"

Cameron gave a low exclamation:

"Then they're headed for more liquor. I thought something was up."

"Is there a cross road back to the Pike?"

"I'm not sure. Probably. I know there is about three miles farther on, almost to the Inn. This is an awful mess to have got you into! I'd rather have been in the guard house than have this happen to you!"

"Please don't!" said Ruth earnestly. "It's an adventure! I'm enjoying it. I'm not a doll to be kept in cotton wool!"

"I should say not!" said Cameron with deep admiration in his tone. "You haven't shown yourself much of a doll to-night. Some doll, to run a car the way you did in the face of all that. I'll tell you better what I think when we get out of this!"

"They are coming, I believe!" said Ruth glancing back. "Don't you see a light? Look!"

Mrs. Cameron was looking, too, through the little back window. Now she spoke quietly:

"Wouldn't it be better to get out and slip up in the woods till they have gone by?"

"No, mother!" said Cameron quickly, "just you sit quiet where you are and trust us."

"Something awful might happen, John!"

"No, mother! Don't you worry!" he said in his gentle, manly tone. Then to Ruth: "There's a big barn ahead there on your left. Keep your eye out for a road around behind it. If we could disappear it's too dark for them to know where we are. Would you care to turn out all the lights and let me run the car? I don't want to boast but there isn't much of anything I can't do with a car when I have to."

Instantly Ruth switched out every light and with a relieved "Please!" gave up the wheel to him. They made the change swiftly and silently, and Ruth took the post of lookout.

"Yes, I can see two lights. It might be someone else, mightn't it?"

"Not likely, on this road. But we're not taking any chances," and with that the car bumped down across a gully and lurched up to a grassy approach to a big stone barn that loomed above them, then slid down another bank and passed close to a great haystack, whose clutching straw fingers reached out to brush their faces, and so swept softly around to the rear of the barn and stopped. Cameron shut off the engine instantly and they sat in utter silence listening to the oncoming car.

"It's they, all right!" whispered Cameron softly. "That's Passmore's voice. He converses almost wholly in choice profanity."

His mother's hand stole out to touch his shoulder and he reached around and held it close.

"Don't tremble, mother, we're all safe!" he whispered in a tone so tender that Ruth felt a shiver of pleasure pass over her for the mother who had such a son. Also there was the instant thought that a man could not be wholly "rotten" when he could speak to his mother in that tone.

There was a breathless space when the car paused on the road not far away and their pursuers stood up and looked around, shouting to one another. There was no mistaking their identity now. Ruth shivered visibly. One of them got out of the car and came toward the barn. They could hear him stepping over the stony roadside. Cameron laid a quiet hand of reassuring protection on her arm that steadied her and made her feel wonderfully safe once more, and strange to say she found herself lifting up another queer little kind of a prayer. It had never been her habit to pray much except in form. Her heart had seldom needed anything that money could not supply.

The man had stumbled across the gully and up toward the barn. They could hear him swearing at the unevenness of the ground, and Ruth held her breath and prayed again. A moment more and he was fumbling about for the barn door and calling for a flash light. Then, like the distant sound of a mighty angel of deliverance came the rumble of a car in the distance. The men heard it and took it for their quarry on ahead. They climbed into their car again and were gone like a flash.

John Cameron did not wait for them to get far away. He set the car in motion as soon as they were out of sight, and its expensive mechanism obeyed his direction almost silently as he guided it around the barn, behind the haystack and back again into the road over which they had just come.

"Now!" he said as he put the car to its best speed and switched on its headlights again. "Now we can beat them to it, I guess, if they come back this way, which I don't think they will."

The car dashed over the ground and the three sat silent while they passed into the woods and over the place where they had first met Cameron. Ruth felt herself trembling again, and her teeth beginning to chatter from the strain. Cameron seemed to realize her feeling and turned toward her:

"You've been wonderful!" he said flashing a warm look at her, "and you, too, mother!" lifting his voice a little and turning his head toward the back seat. "I don't believe any other two women in Bryne Haven could have gone through a scene like that and kept absolutely still. You were great!" There was that in his voice that lifted Ruth's heart more than any praise she had ever received for anything. She wanted to make some acknowledgement, but she found to her surprise that tears were choking her throat so that she could not speak. It was the excitement, of course, she told herself, and struggled to get control of her emotion.

They emerged from the woods and in sight of the Pike at last, and Cameron drew a long breath of relief.

"There, I guess we can hold our own with anyone, now," he said settling back in his seat, but relaxing none of his vigilance toward the car which sped along the highway like a winged thing. "But it's time I heard how you came to be here. I haven't been able to explain it, during the intervals when I've had any chance at all to think about it."

"Oh, I just called up your mother to know if it would help you any to be taken to your train," said Ruth quickly, "and she mentioned that she was worried lest you would miss it; so I suggested that we try to catch you and take you on to Wilmington or Baltimore or wherever you have to go. I do hope this delay hasn't spoiled it all. How long does it take to go from Baltimore to camp. I've taken the Baltimore trip myself in five hours.

It's only quarter past six yet, do you think we can make it?"

"But you can't go all the way to Baltimore!" he exclaimed. "What would you and mother do at that time of night alone after I go to camp? You see, it isn't as if I could stay and come back with you."

"Oh, we'll just go to a hotel in Baltimore, won't we, Mrs. Cameron? We'll be all right if we only get you safe to camp. Do you think we can do it?"

"Oh, yes, we can do it all right with this car. But I'm quite sure I ought not to let you do it just for me. What will your people think?"

"I've left word that I've gone to a friend in trouble," twinkled Ruth. "I'll call them up when I get to Baltimore, and make it all right with Auntie. She will trust me."

Cameron turned and looked at her wonderingly, reverently.

"It's wonderful that you should do this for me," he said in a low tone, quite low, so that the watching wistful mother could not even guess what he was saying.

"It's not in the least wonderful," said Ruth brightly. "Remember the hedge and Chuck Woodcock!" She was beginning to get her self possession again.

"You are paying that old score back in compound interest," said Cameron.

That was a wonderful ride rushing along beneath the stars, going back to childhood's days and getting acquainted again where they left off. Ruth forgot all about the cause of her wild chase, and the two young men she had left disconsolate in her library at home; forgot her own world in this new beautiful one, wherein her spirit really communed with another spirit; forgot utterly what Wainwright had said about Cameron as more and more through their talk she came to see the fineness of his character.

They flashed on from one little village to another, leaving one clustering glimmer of lights in the distance only to pass to other clustering groups. It was in their favor that there were not many other travellers to dispute their way, and they were hindered very little. Cameron had made the trip many times and knew the roads well. They did not have to hesitate and enquire the way. They made good time. The clocks were striking ten when they reached the outskirts of Baltimore.

"Now," said Ruth in a sweetly imperious tone, consulting her timepiece to be sure she had counted the clock strokes correctly, "do you know what you are going to do, Mr. Corporal? You are going to land your mother and me at the nearest hotel, and take the car with you back to camp. You said one of the fellows had his car down there, so I'm sure you'll be able to find a place to put it over night. If you find a way to send the car back to us in the morning, well and good. If not your mother and I will go home by train and the chauffeur can come down to-morrow and bring back the car; or, better still, you can drive yourself up the next time you get leave off."

There was much argument about the matter within a brief space of time, but in the end (which came in five minutes) Ruth had her way, and the young soldier departed for his camp in the gray car with ample time to make the short trip, leaving his mother and Ruth at a Baltimore hotel; after having promised to call up in the morning and let them know what he could do about the car.

Ruth selected a large double room and went at once to the telephone to call up her aunt. She found to her relief that that good lady had not yet returned from her day with a friend in the city, so that no explanations would be necessary that night. She left word with the servant that she was in Baltimore with a friend and would probably be at home the next day sometime. Then she turned to find to her dismay that her companion was sitting in a low armed chair with tears running down her cheeks.

"Oh, my dear!" she exclaimed rushing over to her, "you are all worn out!"

"Not a bit of it!" sobbed the mother with a smile like sunshine through her tears. "I was so happy I couldn't keep from crying. Don't you ever get that way? I've just been watching you and thinking what a dear beautiful child you are and how wonderful God has been to send you to help my boy. Oh, it was so dreadful to me to think of him going down to camp with those men! My dear, I smelt liquor on their breath when they came for him, and I was just crying and praying about it when you called me up. Of course, I knew my boy wouldn't drink, but so many accidents can happen with automobiles when the driver is drunk! My dear, I never can thank you enough!"

They were both too excited to sleep soon, but long after the mother was asleep Ruth lay awake going over the whole day and wondering. There were so many things about the incident of the afternoon and evening, now that they were over, that were utterly out of accord with her whole life heretofore. She felt intuitively that her aunt would never understand if she were to explain the whole proceeding. There were so many laws of her little world of conventionalities that she had transgressed, and so many qualms of a belated conscience about whether she ought to have done it at all. What would Cameron think of her, anyway? Her cheeks burned hot in the dark over that question. Strange she had not thought of it at all either beforehand or while she sat beside him during that wonderful ride! And now the thing that Wainwright had said shouted itself out to her ears: "Rotten! Rotten! Rotten!" like a dirge. Suppose he were? It *couldn't* be true. It *just couldn't,* but suppose he were? Well, suppose he were! How was she hurt by doing a kind act? Having taken that stand against all her former ideas Ruth had instant peace and drifted into dreams of what she had been enjoying, the way suddenly lit by a sleepy remembrance of Wetherill's declaration: "He won't drink! You can't make him! It's been tried again and again!" There was evidence in his favor. Why hadn't she remembered that before? And his mother! She had been so sure of him!

The telephone bell wakened her with a message from camp. His voice greeted her pleasantly with the word that it was all right, he had reached camp in plenty of time, found a good place for the car, and it would be at the hotel at nine o'clock. Ruth turned from the 'phone with a vague disappointment. He had not said a word of thanks or good-bye or anything, only that he must hurry. Not even a word to his mother. But then, of course, men did not think of those little things, perhaps, as women did, and maybe it was just as well for him to take it all as a matter of course. It made it less embarrassing for her.

But when they went down to the car, behold he was in it!

"I got leave off for the morning," he explained smiling. "I told my captain all about how you got me back in time when I'd missed the train and he told me to see you as far as Wilmington and catch the noon train back from there. He's a peach of a captain. If my lieutenant had been there I wouldn't have got a chance to ask him.

I was afraid of that last night. But for good luck the lieutenant has a two days' leave this time. He's a mess!"

Ruth looked at him musingly. Was Harry Wainwright the lieutenant?

They had a golden morning together, and talked of many things that welded a friendship already well begun.

"Weren't you at all frightened last night?" asked Cameron once, looking at the delicate beauty of the face beside him and noting the strength and sweetness of it.

Mrs. Cameron was dosing in the back seat and they felt quite alone and free. Ruth looked up at him frankly:

"Why, yes, I think I was for a minute or two while we were behind that barn, but— Did you ever pray when you were in a trying situation?"

He looked down earnestly into her face, half startled at her words:

"Why, I don't know that I ever did. I'm not quite sure if it was praying."

"Well, I don't know what I ever did before," she went on thoughtfully, "but last night when those men got out of their car in front of the barn so near us again, I found myself praying." She dropped her eyes half embarrassed: "Just as if I were a frightened little child I found myself saying: 'God help us! God help us!' And right away we heard that other car coming and the men went away! It somehow seemed—well, strange! I wondered if anybody else ever had an experience like that."

"I've heard of them," said Cameron gravely. "I've wondered sometimes myself. Do you believe in God?"

"Oh, yes!" said Ruth quite firmly. "Of course. What use would there be in anything if there wasn't a God?"

"But do you believe we humans can ever really— well, *find* Him? On this earth, I mean."

"Why, I don't know that I ever thought about it," she

answered bewildered. "Find Him? In what way do you mean?"

"Why, get in touch with Him? Get to know Him, perhaps. Be on such terms with Him that one could call out in a time like last night, you know; or—well, say in a battle! I've been thinking a lot about that lately—naturally."

"Oh!" gasped Ruth softly, "of course. I hadn't thought about that much, either. We've been so thoughtless—and—and sort of happy you know, just like butterflies, we girls! I haven't realized that men were going out to face *Death!*"

"It isn't that I'm afraid to die," said Cameron proudly lifting his chin as if dying were a small matter, "not just the dying part. I reckon I've been through worse than that a dozen times. That wouldn't last long. It's—the other part. I have a feeling there'll be a little something more expected of me than just to have tried to get the most fun out of life. I've been thinking if there is a God He'd expect us to find it out and make things straight between us somehow. I suppose I don't make myself very plain. I don't believe I know myself just what I mean."

"I think I understand just a little," said Ruth, "I have never thought about it before, but I'm going to now. It's something we ought to think about, I guess. In a sense it's something that each one of us has to think, whether we are going into battle or not, isn't it?"

"I suppose it is, only we never realize it when things are going along all right," said Cameron. "It seems queer that everybody that's ever lived on this earth has had this question to face sooner or later and most of them haven't done much about it. The few people who profess to have found a way to meet it we call cranks, or else pick flaws in the way they live; although it does seem to me that if I really found God so I was sure He was there and cared about me, I'd manage to live a little decenter life than some do."

They drifted into other topics and all too soon they reached Wilmington and had to say good-bye. But the thought stayed with Ruth more or less during the days that followed, and crept into her letters when she wrote to Corporal Cameron, as she did quite often in these days; and still no solution had come to the great question which was so like the one of old, "What shall I do to be saved?" It came and went during the days that followed, and now and again the fact that it had originated in a talk with Cameron clashed badly in her mind with that word "Rotten" that Wainwright had used about him. So that at last she resolved to talk to her cousin, Captain La Rue, the next time he came up.

"Cousin Captain," she said, "do you know a boy at your camp from Bryne Haven named John Cameron?"

"Indeed I do!" said the captain.

"What kind of a man is he?"

"The best young man I know in every way," answered the captain promptly. "If the world were made up of men like him it would be a pretty good place in which to live. Do you know him?"

"A little," said Ruth evasively, with a satisfied smile on her lips. "His mother is in our Red Cross now. She thinks he's about right, of course, but mothers usually do, I guess. I'll have to tell her what you said. It will please her. He used to be in school with me years ago. I haven't seen much of him since."

"Well, all I have to say is, improve your acquaintance if you get the chance. He's worth ten to one of your society youths that loll around here almost every time I come."

"Now, Cousin Captain!" chided Ruth. But she went off smiling and she kept all his words in her heart.

CORPORAL Cameron did not soon return to his native town. An epidemic of measles broke out in camp just before Thanksgiving and pursued its tantalizing course through his special barracks with strenuous vigor. Quarantine was put on for three weeks, and was but lifted for a few hours when a new batch of cases came down. Seven weeks more of isolation followed, when the men were not allowed away from the barracks except for long lonely walks, or gallops across camp. Even the mild excitements of the Y.M.C.A. huts were not for them in these days. They were much shut up to themselves, and latent tendencies broke loose and ran riot. Shooting crap became a passion. They gambled as long as they had a dollar left or could get credit on the next month's pay day. Then they gambled for their shirts and their bayonets. All day long whenever they were in the barracks you could hear the rattle of the dice, and the familiar call of "Phoebe," "Big Dick," "Big Nick" and "Little Joe." When they were not on drill the men would infest the barracks for hours at a time, gathered in crouching groups about the dice, the air thick and blue with cigarette smoke; while others had nothing better to do than to sprawl on their cots and talk; and from their talk Cameron often turned away nauseated. The low ideals, the open boasting of shame, the matter-of-course conviction that all men and most women were as bad as themselves, filled him with a deep boiling rage, and he would close his book or throw down the paper with which he was trying to while the hour, and fling forth into the cold air for a solitary ride or walk.

He was sitting thus a cold cheerless December day with a French book he had recently sent for, trying to study a little and prepare himself for the new country to which he was soon going.

The door of the barracks opened letting in a rush of cold air, and closed again quickly. A tall man in uniform with the red triangle on his arm stood pulling off his woolen gloves and looking about him. Nobody paid any attention to him. Cameron was deep in his book and did not even notice him. Off at his left a new crap game was just starting. The phraseology beat upon his accustomed ears like the buzz of bees or mosquitos.

"I'll shoot a buck!"

"You're faded!"

"Come on now there, dice! Remember the baby's shoes!"

Cameron had ceased to hear the voices. He was struggling with a difficult French idiom.

The stranger took his bearings deliberately and walked over to Cameron, sitting down with a friendly air on the nearest cot.

"Would you be interested in having one of my little books?" he asked, and his voice had a clear ring that brought Cameron's thoughts back to the barracks again. He looked up for a curt refusal. He did not wish to be bothered now, but something in the young man's earnest face held him. Y.M.C.A. men in general were well enough, but Cameron wasn't crazy about them, especially when they were young. But this one had a look about him that proclaimed him neither a slacker nor a sissy. Cameron hesitated:

"What kind of a book?" he asked in a somewhat curt manner.

The boy, for he was only a boy though he was tall as a man, did not hedge but went straight to the point, looking eagerly at the soldier:

"A pocket Testament," he said earnestly, and laid in Cameron's hand a little book with limp leather covers. Cameron took it up half curiously, and then looked into the other's face almost coldly.

"You selling them?" There was a covert sneer in his tone.

"No, no!" said the other quickly, "I'm giving them away for a promise. You see, I had an accident and one of my eyes was put out a while ago. Of course, they wouldn't take me for a soldier, and the next best thing was to be all the help I could to the fellows that are going to fight. I figure that book is the best thing I can bring you."

The manly simplicity of the boy held Cameron's gaze firmly fixed.

"H'm! In what way?" Cameron was turning the leaves curiously, enjoying the silky fineness and the clear-cut print and soft leather binding. Life in the barracks was so much in the rough that any bit of refinement was doubly appreciated. He liked the feel of the little book and had a curious longing to be its possessor.

"Why, it gives you a pretty straight line on where we're all going, what is expected of us, and how we're to be looked out for. It shows one how to know God and be ready to meet death if we have to."

"What makes you think anyone can know God on this earth?" asked Cameron sharply.

"Because *I* have," said the astonishing young man quite as if he were saying he were related to the President or something like that.

"You have! How did you get to know Him?"

"Through that little book and by following it's teachings."

Cameron turned over the pages again, catching familiar phrases here and there as he had heard them sometimes in Sunday school years ago.

"You said something about a promise. What was it?"

"That you'll carry the book with you always, and read at least a verse in it every day."

"Well, that doesn't sound hard," mused Cameron. "I guess I could stand for that."

"The book is yours, then. Would you like to put your name to that acceptance card in the front of the book?"

"What's that?" asked Cameron sharply as if he had discovered the fly in the ointment for which he had all along been suspicious.

"Well, I call it the first step in knowing God. It's your act of acceptance of the way God has planned for you to be forgiven and saved from sin. If you sign that you say you will accept Christ as your Saviour."

"But suppose you don't believe in Christ? I can't commit myself to anything like that till I know about it?"

"Well, you see, that's the first move in getting to know God," said the stranger with a smile. "God says he wants you to believe in His Son. He asks that much of you if you want to get to know Him."

Cameron looked at him with bewildered interest. Was here a possible answer to the questions of his heart. Why did this curious boy have a light in his face that never came from earth or air? What was there about his simple earnestness that was so convincing?

Another crap game had started up on the other side of them. A musically inclined private was playing ragtime on the piano, and another was trying to accompany him on the banjo. The air was hazier than ever. It seemed strange to be talking of such things in these surroundings:

"Let's get out of here and walk!" said Cameron, "I'd like to understand what you mean."

For two hours they tramped across the frozen ground and talked, arguing this way and that, much drawn toward one another. At last in the solemn background of a wall of whispering pines that shut them away from the stark gray rows of barracks, Cameron took out his fountain pen and with his foot on a prone log, opened the little book on his knee and wrote his name and the date. Then he put it in his breast pocket with the solemn feeling that he had taken some kind of a great step toward what his soul had been longing to find. They knelt on the frozen ground beside that log and the stranger prayed simply as if he were talking to a friend. Thereafter that spot was hallowed ground to Cameron, to which he came often to think and to read his little book.

That night he wrote to Ruth, telling in a shy way of his meeting with the Testament man and about the little book. After he had mailed the letter he walked back again to the spot among the pines and standing there looked up to the stars and somehow committed himself again to the covenant he had signed in the little book. It was then that he decided that if he got home again after quarantine before he went over, he would unite with the church. Somehow the stranger's talk that afternoon had cleared away his objections. On his way back to the barracks across the open field, up through the woods and over the crest of the hill toward the road as he walked thinking deeply, suddenly from down below on the road a familiar voice floated up to him. He parted the branches of oak underbrush that made a screen between him and the road and glanced down to get his bearings the better to avoid an unwelcome meeting. It was inevitable when one came near Lieutenant Wainwright that he would overhear some part of a conversation for he had a carrying voice which he never sought to restrain.

"You're sure she's a girl with pep, are you? I don't want to bother with any other kind. All right. Tell her to wait for me in the Washington station to-morrow evening at eight. I'll look for her at the right of the information booth. Tell her to wear a red carnation so I'll know her. I'll show her a good time, all right, if she's the right sort. I'll trust you that she's a good looker!"

Cameron could not hear the response, but the two were standing silhouetted against a distant light, and something in the attitude of the other man held his attention. For a moment he could not place him, then it flashed across his mind that this was the soldier Chambers, who had been the means of his missing the train at Chester on the memorable occasion when Ruth Macdonald had saved the day. It struck him as a strange thing that these two enemies of his whom he would have supposed to be strangers to one another should be talking thus intimately. To make sure of the man's identity he waited until the two parted and Wainwright went his way, and then at a distance followed the other one until he was quite certain. He walked back thoughtfully trying to make it out. Had Wainwright then been at the bottom of his trouble that day? It began to seem quite possible. And how had Ruth Macdonald happened to be so opportunely present at the right moment? How had she happened to turn down that road, a road that was seldom used by people going to Baltimore? It was all very strange and had never been satisfactorily explained. Ruth had evaded the question most plausibly every time he had brought it up. Could it be that Wainwright had told her of a plot against him and she had reached out to help him? His heart leaped at the thought. Then at once he was sure that Wainwright had never told her, unless perhaps he had told some tale against him, and made him the butt of a great joke. Well, if he had she had cared enough to defend him and help him out without ever giving away the fact that she knew. But here, too, lay a thorn to disturb him. Why had Ruth Macdonald not told him the plain truth if she knew? Was she trying to shield Harry Wainwright? Could she really care for that contemptible scoundrel?

The thought in all its phases tore his mind and kept him awake for hours, for the crux of the whole matter was that he was afraid that Ruth Macdonald was going to marry Lieutenant Wainwright, and he knew that it was not only for her sake, but for his also that he did not want this—that it was agony even to contemplate.

He told himself, of course, that his interest was utterly unselfish. That she was nothing to him but a friend and never would be, and that while it might be hard to see her belong to some fine man and know he never might be more than a passing friend, still it would not be like seeing her tied to a rotten unprincipled fellow like Wainwright. The queer part of it was that the word "rotten" in connection with his enemy played a great part in his thoughts that night.

Somewhere in the watches of the night a memory came to him of the covenant he had made that day and a vague wistful reaching of his heart after the Christ to whom he was supposed to have surrendered his life. He wondered if a Christ such as the stranger had claimed He had, would take an interest in the affairs of Ruth Macdonald. Surely, such a flower of a girl would be protected if there was protection for anyone! And somehow he managed a queer little prayer for her, the first he had tried to put up. It helped him a little, and toward morning he fell asleep.

A few days later in glancing through his newly acquired Testament he came upon a verse which greatly troubled him for a time. His eye had caught it at random and somehow it lodged in his mind:

"Forbearing one another, and forgiving one another, if any man have a quarrel against any: even as Christ forgave you, so also do ye."

Somehow the principle of that verse did not fit with his proud spirit. He thought instantly of Wainwright's distasteful face and form. It seemed to loom before him with a smug triumphal sneer. His enmity toward the fellow had been of years standing, and had been deepened many times by unforgetable acts. There was nothing about Wainwright to make one forgive him. There was everything about him to make one want to punish him. When the verse first confronted Cameron he felt a rising indignation that there had been so much as a connection in his thoughts with his quarrel with Wainwright. Why, anybody that knew him knew Wainwright was wrong. God must think so, too. That verse might apply to little quarrels but not to his feeling about the way Wainwright had treated him ever since they were children. That was not to be borne, of course. Those words he had called Cameron's father! How they made his blood boil even now! No, he would not forbear nor forgive Wainwright. God would not want him to do so. It was right he should be against him forever! Thus he dismissed the suggestion and turned to the beginning of his testament, having determined to find the Christ of whom the stranger had set him in search.

On the flyleaf of the little book the stranger had written a few words: ·

> "And ye shall find me, when ye shall search for me with all your heart."—Jeremiah xxix:13.

That meant no half-way business. He could understand that. Well, he was willing to put himself into the search fully. He understood that it was worth a whole-hearted search if one were really to find a God as a reward.

That night he wrote a letter to the minister in Bryne Haven asking for an interview when next he was able to get leave from camp. In the meantime he kept out of the way of Wainwright most adroitly, and found many ways to avoid a meeting.

There had been three awful days when his "peach of a captain" about whom he had spoken to Ruth, had been called away on some military errand and Wainwright had been the commanding officer. They had been days of gall and wormwood to Cameron, for his proud spirit could not bend to salute the man whom he considered a scoundrel, and Wainwright took a fine delight in using his power over his enemy to the limit. If it had not been for the unexpected return of the captain a day earlier than planned, Cameron might have had to suffer humiliations far greater than he did.

The bitterness between the two grew stronger, and Cameron went about with his soul boiling with rage and rebellion. It was only when Ruth's letters came that he forgot it all for a few minutes and lifted his thoughts to higher things.

12

IT was a clear, crisp day in March with just a smell of
Spring in the air, when Cameron finally united with the
church.

He had taken a long time to think about it. Quarantine had extended itself away into February, and while
his company had had its regular drill and hard work,
there had been no leave from camp, no going to
Y.M.C.A. huts, and no visiting canteens. They had been
shut up to the company of the members of their own
barracks, and there were times when that palled upon
Cameron to a distressing degree. Once it had snowed for
three days, and rained on the top of it, and a chill wind
had swept into the cracks and crannies of the barracks,
and poured down from the ventilators in the roofs. The
old stoves were roaring their best to keep up good cheer,
and the men lay on their cots in rows talking; telling their
vile stories, one after another, each to sound bigger than
the last, some mere lads boasting of wild orgies, and all
finally drifting into a chat on a sort of philosophy of the
lowest ideals. Cameron lay on his cot trying to sleep, for
he had been on guard all night, and a letter from Ruth

was in his inside pocket with a comfortable crackle, but the talk that drifted about him penetrated even his army blankets when he drew them up over his ears.

The fellows had arrived at a point where a young lad from Texas had stated with a drawl that all girls were more or less bad; that this talk of the high standards of womanhood was all bosh; that there was one standard for men and women, yes, but it was man's standard, not woman's, as was written sometimes. White womanhood! Bah! There was no such thing!

In vain Cameron stuffed the blanket about his ears, resolutely shut his eyes and tried to sleep. His very blood boiled in his veins. The letter in his pocket cried out to be exonerated from this wholesale blackening. Suddenly Cameron flung the blanket from him and sprang to his feet with a single motion, a tall soldier with a white flame of wrath in his face, his eyes flashing with fire. They called him in friendly derision the "Silent Corporal" because he kept so much to himself, but now he blazed forth at them:

"You lie Kelly! You know you do! The whole lot of you are liars! You know that rot you've been talking isn't true. You know that it's to cover up your own vile deeds and to excuse your own lustful passions that you talk this way and try to persuade your hearts and consciences that you are no worse than the girls you have dishonored! But it isn't so and you know it! There *are* good women! There always have been and there always will be! You, every one of you, know at least one. You are dishonoring your mothers and your sisters when you talk that way. You are worse than the beasts you are going out to fight. That's the rotten stuff they are teaching. They call it Kultur! You'll never win out against them if you go in that spirit, for it's their spirit and nothing more. You've got to go clean! If there's a God in heaven He's in this war, and it's got to be a clean war! And you've got to begin by thinking differently of women or you're just as bad as the Huns!"

With that he seized his poncho, stamped out into the storm, and tramped for two hours with a driving sleet in his face, his thoughts a fury of holy anger against unholy things, and back of it all the feeling that he was the knight of true womanhood. She had sent him forth and no man in his presence should defile the thought of her. It was during that tramp that he had made up his mind to ally himself with God's people. Whether it would do any good in the long run in his search for God or not, whether he even was sure he believed in God or not, he would do that much if he were permitted.

His interview with the minister had not made things much plainer. He had been told that he would grow into things. That the church was the shepherd-fold of the soul, that he would be nurtured and taught, that by and by these doubts and fears would not trouble him. He did not quite see it, how he was to be nurtured on the distant battlefield of France, but it was a mystical thing, anyway, and he accepted the statement and let it go at that. One thing that stuck in his heart and troubled him deeply was the way the minister talked to him about love and fellowship with his fellow men. As a general thing, Cameron had no trouble with his companions in life, but there were one or two, notably Wainwright and a young captain friend of his at camp, named Wurtz, toward whom his enmity almost amounted to hatred.

He was not altogether sure that the minister's suggestion that he might love the sinner and hate the sin would hold good with regard to Wainwright; but there had been only a brief time before the communion service and he had had to let the matter go. His soul was filled with a holy uplifting as he stepped out from the pastor's study and followed into the great church.

It had startled him just a little to find so many people there. In contemplating this act of allying himself with God he had always thought of it as being between himself and God, with perhaps the minister and an elder or two. He sat down in the place indicated for him much disturbed in spirit. It had always been an annoyance to him to be brought to the notice of his fellow townsmen, and a man in uniform in these days was more than ever an object of interest. His troubled gaze was downward during the opening hymns and prayers. But when he came to stand and take his vows he lifted his eyes, and there, off at one side where the seats grouped in a sort of transept, he caught a glimpse of Ruth Macdonald standing beside her tall Captain-cousin who was home for the day, and there was a light in her eyes that steadied him and brought back the solemnity of the moment once more. It thrilled him to think she was there. He had not realized before that this must be her church. In fact, he had not thought of it as being any church in particular, but as being a part of the great church invisible to which all God's children belonged. It had not occurred to him until that morning, either, that his mother might be hurt that he had not chosen her church. But when he spoke to her about it she shook her head and smiled. She was only glad of what he was doing. There were no regrets. She was too broad minded to stop about creeds. She was sitting there meekly over by the wall now, her hands folded quietly in her lap, tears of joy in her eyes. She, too, had seen Ruth Macdonald and was glad, but she wondered who the tall captain by her side might be.

It happened that Cameron was the only person uniting by confession at that time, for the quarantine had held him beyond the time the pastor had spoken of when so many were joining, and he stood alone, tall and handsome in his uniform, and answered in a clear, deep voice: "I do," "I will!" as the vows were put upon him one by one. Every word he meant from his heart, a longing for the God who alone could satisfy the longings of his soul.

He thrilled with strange new enthusiasm as the congregation of church members were finally called upon to rise and receive him into their fellowship, and looking across he saw Ruth Macdonald again and his beloved Captain La Rue standing together while everybody sang:

> Blest be the tie that binds
> Our hearts in Christian love;
> The fellowship of kindred minds
> Is like to that above.

But when the bread and the wine had been partaken of, the solemn prayer of dedication spoken, the beautiful service was over, and the rich tones of the organ were swelling forth, he suddenly felt strange and shy among all that crowd of people whom he knew by sight only. The elders and some of the other men and women shook hands with him, and he was trying to slip away and find his mother when a kindly hand was laid upon his shoulder and there stood the captain with Ruth beside him, and a warm hand shake of welcome into the church.

"I'm so glad," he said, "that you have taken this step. You will never regret it, Cameron. It is good that we can be of the same company here if we have failed in other ways." Then turning to Ruth he said:

"I didn't tell you, did I, Ruth, that I've failed in trying to get Cameron transferred to my division? I did everything I could, but they've turned down my application flatly. It seems like stupidity to me, for it was just the place for which he was most fitted, but I guess it's because he was too much of a man to stay in a quiet sector and do such work. If he had been maimed or half blinded they might have considered him. They need him in his present place, and I am the poorer for it."

There was a glow in Ruth's eyes as she put her hand in Cameron's and said simply: "I'm glad you're one of us now," that warmed his heart with a great gladness.

"I didn't know you were a member," he said wonderingly.

"Why, yes, I've been a member since I was fourteen," she said, and suddenly he felt that he had indeed come into a holy and blessed communion. If he had not yet found God, at least he was standing on the same ground with one of his holy children.

That was the last time he got home before he sailed. Shipping quarantine was put on his company the very next week, the camp was closed to visitors, and all passes annulled. The word came that they would be going over in a few days, but still they lingered, till the days grew into three weeks, and the Spring was fully upon them in all its beauty, touching even the bare camp with a fringe of greenness and a sprinkle of wild bloom in the corners where the clearing had not been complete.

Added to his other disappointments, a direful change had taken place at camp. The "peach of a captain" had been raised to the rank of major and Captain Wurtz had been put in his place. It seemed as if nothing worse could be.

The letters had been going back and forth rather often of late, and Cameron had walked to the loneliest spot in the camp in the starlight and had it out with himself. He knew now that Ruth Macdonald was the only girl in all the world to him. He also knew that there was not a chance in a thousand that he could ever be more to her than he now was. He knew that the coming months held pain for him, and yet, he would not go back and undo this beautiful friendship, no, not for all the pain that might come. It was worth it, every bit.

He had hoped to get one more trip home, and she had wanted to see the camp, had said that perhaps when the weather got warmer she might run down some day with his mother, but now the quarantine was on and that was out of the question. He walked alone to the places he would have liked to show her, and then with a sigh went to the telephone office and waited two hours till he got a connection through to her house, just to tell her how sorry he was that he could not come up as he had expected and take that ride with her that she had promised in her last letter. Somehow it comforted him to hear her voice. She had asked if there would no lifting of the quarantine before they left, no opportunity to meet him somewhere and say good-bye, and he promised that he would let her know if any such chance came; but he had little hope, for company after company were being sent away in the troop trains now, hour after hour, and he might be taken any minute.

Then one day he called her up and told her that the next Saturday and Sunday the camp was to be thrown open to visitors, and if she could come down with his mother he would meet them at the Hostess' House and they could spend the day together. Ruth promptly accepted the invitation and promised to arrange it all with his mother and take the first train down Saturday morning. After he had hung up the receiver and paid his bill he walked away from the little telephone headquarters in a daze of joy. She had promised to come! For one whole day he would have her to himself! She was willing to come with his mother! Then as he passed the officers' headquarters it occurred to him that perhaps she had other interests in coming to camp than just to see him, and he frowned in the darkness and his heart burned hot within him. What if they should meet Wainwright! How the day would be spoiled!

With this trouble on his mind he went quite early in the morning down as near to the little trolley station as he could get, for since the quarantine had been put on no soldiers without a special pass were allowed beyond a certain point, which was roped off about the trolley station. Sadly, Cameron took his place in the front rank, and stood with folded arms to wait. He knew he would have some time to stand before he could look for his guests, but the crowd was always so great at the train times that it was well to get a good place early. So he stood and thought his sad thoughts, almost wishing he had not asked them to come, as he realized more and more what unpleasantness might arise in case Wainwright should find out who were his guests. He was sure that the lieutenant was not above sending him away on a foolish errand, or getting him into a humiliating situation before his friends.

As he stood thus going over the situation and trying to plan how he might spirit his guests away to some pleasant spot where Wainwright would not be likely to penetrate, he heard the pompous voice of the lieutenant himself, and slipping behind a comrade turned his face away so that he would not be recognized.

"Yes, I got special leave for three days!" proclaimed the satisfied voice, and Cameron's heart bounded up so joyously that he would have almost been willing then and there to put aside his vow not to salute him, and throw his arms about his enemy. Going away for three days. That meant two things! First that Wainwright would not have to be thought of in making his plans, and second that they were evidently not going to move before Wainwright got back. They surely would not have given him leave if the company was to be sent away that day. A third exultant thought followed; Wainwright was going home presumably to see Ruth and Ruth would not be there! Perhaps, oh *perhaps* he might be able to persuade her and his mother to stay over Sunday! He hardly dared to hope, however, for Ruth Macdonald might think it presumptuous in him to suggest it, and again she might wish to go home to meet Wainwright. And, too, where could they sleep if they did stay. It was hopeless, of course. They would have to go back to Baltimore or to Washington for the night and that would be a hard jaunt.

However, Ruth Macdonald had thought of such a possibility herself, and when she and Mrs. Cameron stepped down from the Philadelphia train at the small country station that had suddenly become an important point because of the great camp that had sprung up within a stone's throw of it, she looked around enquiringly at the little cottage homes in sight and said to her companion:

"Would it be very dreadful in us to discover if there is some place here where we could stay over night in case John's company does not go just yet and we find we would be allowed to see him again on Sunday?"

She knew by the sudden lighting of the mother's wistful face that she had read aright the sighs half stifled that she had heard on the train when the mother had thought she was not noticing.

"Oh, do you suppose we could stay?" The voice was full of yearning.

"Well, we can find out, at least. Anyhow, I'm going

in here to see whether they would take us in case we could. It looks like a nice neat place."

Ruth pulled open the gate, ran up the steps of the pleasant porch shaded with climbing roses, and knocked timidly at the open door.

A broad, somewhat frowsy woman appeared and surveyed her coolly with that apprising glance that a native often gives to a stranger; took in the elegant simplicity of her quiet expensive gown and hat, lingering with a jealous glance on the exquisite hand bag she carried, then replied apathetically to Ruth's question:

"No, we're all full. We ain't got any room. You might try down to the Salvation Army Hut. They got a few rooms down there. It's just been built. They might take you in. It's down the road a piece, that green building to the right. You can't miss it. You'll see the sign."

Ruth caught her breath, thanked her and hastened back to her companion. Salvation Army! That was eccentric, queer, but it would be perfectly respectable! Or would it? Would Aunt Rhoda disapprove very much? Somehow the Salvation Army was associated in her mind with slums and drunkards. But, at least, they might be able to direct her to a respectable place.

Mrs. Cameron, too, looked dubious. This having a society girl to chaperone was new business for her. She had never thought much about it, but somehow she would hardly have associated the Salvation Army with the Macdonald family in any way. She paused and looked doubtfully at the unpretentious little one-story building that stretched away capaciously and unostentatiously from the grassy roadside.

"Salvation Army" arose in bold inviting letters from the roof, and "Ice Cold Lemonade" beckoned from a sign on the neat screen door. Ruth was a bit excited.

"I'm going in!" she declared and stepped within the door, Mrs. Cameron following half fearfully.

The room which they entered was long and clean and pleasant. Simple white curtains draped the windows, many rush-bottomed big rocking chairs were scattered about, a long desk or table ran along one side of the room with writing materials, a piano stood open with music on its rack, and shelves of books and magazines filled the front wall.

Beyond the piano were half a dozen little tables, white topped and ready for a hungry guest. At the back a counter ran the width of the room, with sandwiches and pies under glass covers, and a bright coffee urn steaming suggestively at one end. Behind it through an open door was a view of the kitchen, neat, handy, crude, but all quite clean, and through this door stepped a sweet-faced woman, wiping her hands on her gingham apron and coming toward them with a smile of welcome as if they were expected guests. It was all so primitive, and yet there was something about it that bore the dignity of refinement, and puzzled this girl from her sheltered home. She was almost embarrassed to make her enquiry, but the hearty response put her quite at her ease, as if she had asked a great favor of another lady in a time of stress:

"I'm so sorry, but our rooms are all taken," the woman waved a slender hand toward the long side of the room and Ruth noticed for the first time that a low partition ran the length of the room at one side with doors. Mechanically she counted them, eight of them, neat, gray-painted doors. Could these be rooms? How interesting! She had a wild desire to see inside them. Rooms! They were more like little stalls, for the partitions did not reach all the way to the ceiling. A vision of her own spacious apartment at home came floating in vague contrast. Then one of the doors opposite her opened as its occupant, a quiet little elderly woman, came out, and she had a brief glimpse of the white curtained window, the white draped comfortable looking bed, a row of calico curtained hooks on the wall, and a speck of a wash stand with tin pitcher and basin in the corner, all as clean and new as the rest of the place. She swiftly decided to stay here if there was any chance. Another look at the sweet face of the presiding woman who was trying to make them understand how crowded everything was, and how many mothers there were with sons who were going that night or the next, and who wanted to be near them, determined her. She was saying there was just a chance in case a certain mother from Boston who had written her did not arrive at five o'clock:

"But we ought not to take a chance," said Cameron's mother, looking at the eager faced girl with a cautious wistfulness. "What could we do if night came and we had no place to stay?"

Ruth cast her eyes about.

"Couldn't we sit in a couple of those rocking chairs all night?" she asked eagerly.

The Salvation Army woman laughed affectionately as if she had found a kindred spirit:

"Why, dearie, I could give you a couple of cots out here in the dining room if you didn't mind. I wouldn't have pillows, but I think I could get you some blankets."

"Then we'll stay," said Ruth triumphantly before Mrs. Cameron could protest, and went away feeling that she had a new friend in the wise sweet Salvation Army woman. In five minutes more they were seated in the trolley on their way into the camp.

"I'm afraid your people would not like you to stay in such a place," began Mrs. Cameron dubiously, though her eyes shone with a light that belied her words.

"Nonsense!" said Ruth with a bewildering smile, "it is as clean as a pin and I'm very much excited about staying there. It will be an adventure. I've never known much about the Salvation Army before, except that they are supposed to be very good people."

"There might be some rough characters—"

"Well, I guess they can't hurt us with that good woman around, and anyhow, you're going to stay till your son goes!" laughingly declared Ruth.

"Well, we'll see what John says," said his mother with a sigh, "I can't let you do anything—questionable."

"Please, Mrs. Cameron," pleaded Ruth, "let us forget things like that this trip and just have a happy time."

The mother smiled, sadly, wistfully, through a mist of tears. She could not help thinking how wonderful it would have been if there had been no war and her dear boy could have had this sweet wholesome girl for a friend.

13

THE sun was shining gloriously when the two stepped from the trolley at the little camp station and looked bewildered about them at the swarms of uniforms and boyish faces, searching for their one. They walked through the long lane lined with soldiers, held back by the great rope and guarded by Military Police. Each crowding eager soldier had an air of expectancy upon him, a silence upon him that showed the realization of the parting that was soon to be. In many faces deep disappointment was growing as the expected ones did not arrive. Ruth's throat was filled with oppression and tears as she looked about and suddenly felt the grip of war, and realized that all these thousands were bearing this bitterness of parting, perhaps forever. Death stalking up and down a battlefield, waiting to take his pick of them! This was the picture that flashed before her shrinking eyes.

It was almost like a solemn ceremony, this walking down the lane of silent waiting soldiers, to be claimed by their one. It seemed to bring the two young people nearer in heart than they had ever been before, when at the end of the line Cameron met them with a salute, kissed his mother, and then turned to Ruth and took her hand with an earnest grave look of deep pleasure in his eyes.

He led them up under the big trees in front of the Hostess' House while all around were hushed voices, and teary eyes. That first moment of meeting was the saddest and the quietest of the day with everybody, except the last parting hour when mute grief sat unchecked upon every face, and no one stopped to notice if any man were watching, but just lived out his real heart self, and showed his mother or his sister or his sweetheart how much he loved and suffered.

That was a day which all the little painted butterflies of temptation should have been made to witness. There were no painted ladies coming through the gates that day. This was no time for friendships like that. Death was calling, and the deep realities of life stood out and demanded attention.

The whole thing was unlike anything Ruth had ever witnessed before. It was a new world. It was as if the old conventions which had heretofore hedged her life were dropped like a garment revealing life as it really was, and every one walked unashamed, because the great sorrow and need of all had obliterated the little petty rules of life, and small passions were laid aside, while hearts throbbed in a common cause.

He waited on them like a prince, seeming to anticipate every need, and smooth every annoyance. He led them away from the throng to the quiet hillside above the camp where spring had set her dainty foot-print. He spread down his thick army blanket for them to sit upon and they held sweet converse for an hour or two. He told them of camp life and what was expected to be when they started over, and when they reached the other side.

His mother was brave and sensible. Sometimes the tears would brim over at some suggestion of what her boy was soon to bear or do, but she wore a smile as courageous and sweet as any saint could wear. The boy saw and grew tender over it. A bird came and sang over their heads, and the moment was sweet with springing things and quiet with the brooding tenderness of parting that hung over the busy camp. Ruth had one awful moment of adjustment when she tried to think how her aunt Rhoda would look if she could see her now; then she threw the whole thing to the winds and resolved to enjoy the day. She saw that while the conventions by which she had been reared were a good thing in general, perhaps, they certainly were not meant to hamper or hinder the true and natural life of the heart, or, if they were, they were not *good* things; and she entered into the moment with her full sympathy. Perhaps Aunt Rhoda would not understand, but the girl she had brought up knew that it was good to be here. Her aunt was away from home with an invalid friend on a short trip so there had been no one to question Ruth's movements when she decided to run down to Washington with a "friend from the Red Cross" and incidentally visit the camp a little while.

He had them over the camp by and by, to the trenches and dummies, and all the paraphernalia of war prepara- tion. Then they went back to the Hostess' House and fell into line to get dinner. As Cameron stood looking down at Ruth in the crowded line in the democratic way which was the only way there was, it came over them both how strange and wonderful it was that they two who had seen each other so little in their lives and who had come from such widely separated social circles should be there together in that beautiful intimacy. It came to them both at once and flashed its thought from one pair of eyes to the other and back again. Cameron looked deep into her thoughts then for a moment to find out if there was a shadow of mortification or dismay in her face; but though she flushed consciously her sweet true eyes gave back only the pleasure she was feeling, and her real enjoyment of the day. Then instantly each of them felt that another crisis had been passed in their friendship, another something unseen and beautiful had happened that made this moment most precious—one never to be forgotten no matter what happened in the future, something they would not have missed for any other experience.

It was Ruth who announced suddenly, late in the afternoon, during a silence in which each one was thinking how fast the day was going:

"Did you know that we were going to stay over Sunday?"

Cameron's face blazed with joyful light:

"Wonderful!" he said softly, "do you mean it? I've been trying to get courage all day to suggest it, only I don't know of any place this side of Washington or Baltimore where you can be comfortable, and I hate to think of you hunting around a strange city late at night for accommodations. If I could only get out to go with you—!"

"It isn't necessary," said Ruth quickly, "we have our accommodations all arranged for. Your mother and I planned it all out before we came. But are you sure we can get into camp to-morrow?"

"Yes, I'm almost certain we can get you passes by going up to officers' headquarters and applying. A fellow in our company told me this morning he had permission for his mother and sister to come in to-morrow. And we are not likely to leave before Monday now, for this morning our lieutenant went away and I heard him say he had a three days' leave. They wouldn't have given him that if they expected to send us before he got back, at least not unless they recalled him—they might do that."

"Is that the lieutenant that you called a 'mess' the other day?" asked Ruth with twinkling eyes.

"Yes," said Cameron turning a keen, startled glance at her, and wondering what she would say if she knew it was Wainwright he meant.

But she answered demurely:

"So he's away, is he? I'm glad. I was hoping he would be."

"Why?" asked Cameron.

"Oh, I thought he might be in the way," she smiled, and changed the subject, calling attention to the meadow lark who was trilling out his little ecstasy in the tall tree over their head.

Cameron gave one glance at the bird and then brought his gaze back to the sweet upturned face beside him, his soul thrilling with the wonder of it that she should be there with him!

"But you haven't told me where you have arranged to stay. Is it Baltimore or Washington? I must look up your trains. I hope you will be able to stay as late as possible. They're not putting people out of camp until eight o'clock to-night."

"Lovely!" said Ruth with the eagerness of a child. "Then we'll stay till the very last trolley. We're not going to either Baltimore or Washington. We're staying right near the camp entrance in that little town at the station where we landed, I don't remember what you call it. We got accommodations this morning before we came into camp."

"But where?" asked Cameron anxiously. "Are you sure it's respectable? I'm afraid there isn't any place there that would do at all."

"Oh, yes there is," said Ruth. "It's the Salvation Army 'Hut,' they called it, but it looks more like a barracks, and there's the dearest little woman in charge!"

"John, I'm afraid it isn't the right thing to let her do it!" put in his mother anxiously. "I'm afraid her aunt wouldn't like it at all, and I'm sure she won't be comfortable."

"I shall *love* it!" said Ruth happily, "and my aunt will never know anything about it. As for comfort, I'll be as comfortable as you are, my dear lady, and I'm sure you wouldn't let comfort stand in the way of being with your boy." She smiled her sweet little triumph that brought tears to the eyes of the mother; and Cameron gave her a blinding look of gratitude and adoration. So she carried her way.

Cameron protested no more, but quietly enquired at the Hostess' House if the place was all right, and when he put them on the car at eight o'clock he gave Ruth's hand a lingering pressure, and said in a low tone that only she could hear, with a look that carried its meaning to her heart:

"I shall never forget that you did this for my mother—and me!"

The two felt almost light-hearted in comparison to their fellow travellers, because they had a short reprieve before they would have to say good-bye. But Ruth sat looking about her, at the sad-eyed girls and women who had just parted from their husbands and sons and sweethearts, and who were most of them weeping, and felt anew the great burden of the universal sorrow upon her. She wondered how God could stand it. The old human question that wonders how God can stand the great agonies of life that have to come to cure the world of its sin, and never wonders how God can stand the sin! She felt as if she must somehow find God and plead with Him not to do it, and again there came that longing to her soul, if she only knew God intimately! Cameron's question recurred to her thoughts, *"Could* anyone on this earth know God? Had anyone ever known Him? Would the Bible say anything about it?" She resolved to read it through and find out.

The brief ride brought them suddenly into a new and to Ruth somewhat startling environment.

As they followed the grassy path from the station to their abiding place two little boys in full military uniform appeared out of the tall grass of the meadows, one as a private, the other as an officer. The small private saluted the officer with precision and marched on, turning after a few steps to call back, "Mother said we might sleep in the tent to-night! The rooms are all full." The older boy gave a whoop of delight and bounded back toward the building with a most unofficer-like walk, and both disappeared inside the door. A tiny khaki dog-tent was set up in the grass by the back door, and in a moment more the two young soldiers emerged from the back door with blankets and disappeared under the brown roof with a zest that showed it was no hardship to them to camp out for the night.

There were lights in the long pleasant room, and people. Two soldiers with their girls were eating ice cream at the little tables, and around the piano a group of officers and their wives was gathered singing ragtime. Ruth's quick glance told her they were not the kind she cared for, and—how could people who were about to part, perhaps forever, stand there and sing such abominable nonsense! Yet—perhaps it was their way of being brave to the last. But she wished they would go.

The sweet-faced woman of the morning was busy behind the counter and presently she saw them and came forward:

"I'm sorry! I hoped there would be a room, but that woman from Boston came. I can only give you cots out here, if you don't mind."

Mrs. Cameron looked around in a half-frightened manner, but Ruth smiled airily and said that would be all right.

They settled down in the corner between the writing table and book case and began to read, for it was obvious that they could not retire at present.

The little boys came running through and the officers corralled them and clamored for them to sing. Without any coaxing they stood up together and sang, and their voices were sweet as birds as they piped out the words of a popular song, one singing alto, the little one taking the high soprano. Ruth put down her book and listened, wondering at the lovely expressions on the two small faces. They made her think of the baby-seraphs in Michaelangelo's pictures. Presently they burst into a religious song with as much gusto as they had sung the ragtime. They were utterly without self-consciousness, and sang with the fervor of a preacher. Yet they were regular boys, for presently when they were released they went to turning hand springs and had a rough and tumble scuffle in the corner till their mother called them to order.

In a few minutes more the noisy officers and their wives parted, the men striding off into the night with a last word about the possibility of unexpected orders coming, and a promise to wink a flash light out of the car window as the troop train went by in case they went out that night. The wives went into one of the little stall-rooms and compared notes about their own feelings and the probability of the -Nth Division leaving before Monday.

Then the head of the house appeared with a Bible under his arm humming a hymn. He cast a keen pleasant glance at the two strangers in the corner, and gave a cheery word to his wife in answer to her question:

"Yes, we had a great meeting to-night. A hundred and twenty men raised their hands as wanting to decide for Christ, and two came forward to be prayed for. It was a blessed time. I wish the boys had been over there to sing. The meeting was in the big Y.M.C.A. auditorium. Has Captain Hawley gone yet?"

"Not yet." His wife's voice was lowered. She motioned toward one of the eight gray doors, and her husband nodded sadly.

"He goes at midnight, you know. Poor little woman!"

Just then the door opened and a young soldier came out, followed by his wife, looking little and pathetic with great dark hollows under her eyes, and a forced smile on her trembling lips.

The soldier came over and took the hand of the Salvation Army woman:

"Well, I'm going out to-night, Mother. I want to thank you for all you've done for my little girl"—looking toward his wife—"and I won't forget all the good things you've done for *me,* and the sermons you've preached; and when I get over there I'm going to try to live right and keep all my promises. I want you to pray for me that I may be true. I shall never cease to thank the Lord that I knew you two."

The Salvationists shook hands earnestly with him, and promised to pray for him, and then he turned to the children:

"Good-bye, Dicky, I shan't forget the songs you've

sung. I'll hear them sometimes when I get over there in battle, and they'll help to keep me true."

But Dicky, not content with a hand shake swarmed up the leg and back of his tall friend as if he had been a tree, and whispered in a loud confidential child-whisper:

"I'm a goin' to pray fer you, too, Cap'n Hawley. God bless you!"

The grown-up phrases on the childish lips amused Ruth. She watched the little boy as he lifted his beautiful serious face to the responsive look of the stranger, and marvelled. Here was no parrot-like repetition of word she had heard oft repeated by his elders; the boy was talking a native tongue, and speaking of things that were real to him. There was no assumption of godliness nor conceit, no holier-than-thou smirk about the child. It was all sincere, as a boy would promise to speak to his own father about a friend's need. It touched Ruth and tears sprang to her eyes.

All the doubts she had had about the respectability of the place had vanished long ago. There might be all kinds of people coming and going, but there was a holy influence here which made it a refuge for anyone, and she felt quite safe about sleeping in the great barn-like room so open. It was as if they had happened on some saint's abode and been made welcome in their extremity.

Presently, one by one the inmates of the rooms came in and retired. Then the cots were brought out and set up, little simple affairs of canvas and steel rods, put together in a twinkling, and very inviting to the two weary women after the long day. The cheery proprietor called out, "Mrs. Brown, haven't you an extra blanket in your room?" and a pleasant voice responded promptly, "Yes, do you want it?"

"Throw it over then, please. A couple of ladies hadn't any place to go. Anybody else got one?"

A great gray blanket came flying over the top of the partition, and down the line another voice called: "I have one I don't need!" and a white blanket with pink stripes followed, both caught by the Salvationist, and spread upon the little cots. Then the lights were turned out one by one and there in the shelter of the tall piano, curtained by the darkness the two lay down.

Ruth was so interested in it all and so filled with the humor and the strangeness of her situation that tired as she was she could not sleep for a long time.

The house settled slowly to quiet. The proprietor and his wife talked comfortably about the duties of the next day, called some directions to the two boys in the puppy tent, soothed their mosquito bites with a lotion and got them another blanket. The woman who helped in the kitchen complained about not having enough supplies for morning, and that contingency was arranged for, all in a patient, earnest way and in the same tone in which they talked about the meetings. They discussed their own boy, evidently the brother of the small boys, who had apparently just sailed for France as a soldier a few days before, and whom the wife had gone to New York to see off, and they commended him to their Christ in little low sentences of reassurance to each other. Ruth could not help but hear much that was said, for the rooms were all open to sounds, and these good people apparently had nothing to hide. They spoke as if all their household were one great family, equally interested in one another, equally suffering and patient in the necessities of this awful war.

In another tiny room the Y.M.C.A. man who had been the last to come in talked in low tones with his wife, telling her in tender, loving tones what to do about a number of things after he was gone.

In a room quite near there were soft sounds as of

GRACE LIVINGSTON HILL

suppressed weeping. Something made Ruth sure it was the mother who had been spoken of earlier in the evening as having come all the way from Texas and arrived too late to bid her boy good-bye.

Now and again the sound of a troop train stirred her heart to untold depths. There is something so weird and sorrowful about its going, as if the very engine sympathized, screaming its sorrow through the night. Ruth felt she never would forget that sound. Out there in the dark Cameron might be even then slipping past them out into the great future. She wished she could dare ask that sweet faced woman, or that dear little boy to pray for *him*. Maybe she would next day.

The two officer's wives seemed to sit up in bed and watch the train. They had discovered a flash light, and were counting the signals, and quite excited. Ruth's heart ached for them. It was a peculiarity of this trip that she found her heart going out to others so much more than it had ever gone before. She was not thinking of her own pain, although she knew it was there, but of the pain of the world.

Her body lying on the strange hard cot ached with weariness in unaccustomed places, yet she stretched and nestled upon the tan canvas with satisfaction. She was sharing to a certain extent the hardships of the soldiers— the hardship of one soldier whose privations hurt her deeply. It was good to have to suffer—with him. Where was God? Did He care? Was He in this queer little hostel? Might she ask Him now to set a guard over Cameron and let him find the help he needed wherewith to go to meet Death, if Death he must meet?

She laid her hands together as a little child might do and with wide-open eyes staring into the dark of the high ceiling she whispered from her heart: "Oh God,

146

help—*us*—to find *you!*" and unconsciously she, too, set her soul on the search that night.

As she closed her eyes a great peace and sense of safety came over her.

Outside on the road a company of late soldiers, coming home from leave noised by. Some of them were drunk, and wrangling or singing, and a sense of their pitiful need of God came over her as she sank into a deep sleep.

14

SHE was awakened by the rattling of the pots and pans in the tiny kitchen. She sat up startled and looked about her. It was very early. The first sunlight was streaming redly through the window screens, and the freshness of the morning was everywhere, for all the windows were wide open. The stillness of the country, broken only by the joyous chorus of the birds, struck her as a wonderful thing. She lay down again and closed her eyes to listen. Music with the scent of clover! The cheery little home noises in the kitchen seemed a pleasant background for the peace of the Sabbath morning. It was so new and strange. Then came the thought of camp and the anticipation of the day, with the sharp pang at the memory that perhaps even now Cameron was gone. Orders were so uncertain. In the army a man must be ready to move at a moment's notice. What if while she slept he had passed by on one of those terrible troop trains!

She sat up again and began to put her hair into order and make herself presentable. He had promised that if such a thing as a sudden move should occur he would throw out an old envelope with his name written on it as they passed by the hut, and she meant to go out to that railroad track and make a thorough search before the general public were up.

Mrs. Cameron was still sleeping soundly, one work-worn hand partly shading her face. Ruth knew instinctively that she must have been weeping in the night. In the early morning dawn she drooped on the hard little cot in a crumpled heap, and the girl's heart ached for her sorrow.

Ruth stole into the kitchen to ask for water to wash her face:

"I'm sorry," said the pleasant-faced woman who was making coffee and frying bacon, "but the wash basins are all gone; we've had so many folks come in. But you can have this pail. I just got this water for myself and I'll let you have it and I'll get some more. You see, the water pipes aren't put in the building yet and we have to go down the road quite a piece to get any. This is all there was left last night."

She handed Ruth a two-gallon galvanized tin bucket containing a couple of inches of water, obviously clean, and added a brief towel to the toilet arrangements.

Ruth beat a hasty retreat back to the shelter of the piano with her collection, fearing lest mirth would get the better of her. She could not help thinking how her aunt would look if she could see her washing her face in this pittance of water in the bottom of the great big bucket.

But Ruth Macdonald was adaptable in spite of her upbringing. She managed to make a most pleasing toilet in spite of the paucity of water, and then went back to the kitchen with the bucket.

"If you will show me where you get the water I'll go for some more," she offered, anxious for an excuse to get out and explore the track.

The woman in the kitchen was not abashed at the offer. She accepted the suggestion as a matter of course, taking for granted the same helpful spirit that seemed to pervade all the people around the place. It did not seem to strike her as anything strange that this young woman should be willing to go for water. She was not giving attention to details like clothes and handbags, and neither wealth nor social station belonged to her scheme of life. So she smilingly gave the directions to the pump and went on breaking nice brown eggs into a big yellow bowl. Ruth wished she could stay and watch, it looked so interesting.

She took the pail and slipped out the back door, but before she went in search of water she hurried down to the railroad track and scanned it for several rods either way, carefully examining each bit of paper, her breath held in suspense as she turned over an envelope or scrap of paper, lest it might bear his name. At last with a glad look backward to be sure she had missed nothing, she hurried up the bank and took her way down the grassy path toward the pump, satisfied that Cameron had not yet left the camp.

It was a lovely summer morning, and the quietness of the country struck her as never before. The wild roses shimmered along the roadside in the early sun, and bees and butterflies were busy about their own affairs. It seemed such a lovely world if it only had not been for *war*. How could God bear it! She lifted her eyes to the deep blue of the sky, where little clouds floated lazily, like lovely aviators out for pleasure. Was God up there? If she might only find Him. What did it all mean, anyway? Did He really care for individuals?

It was all such a new experience, the village pump, and the few early stragglers watching her curiously from the station platform. A couple of grave soldiers hurried by, and the pang of what was to come shot through her heart. The thought of the day was full of mingled joy and sorrow.

They ate a simple little breakfast, good coffee, toast and fried eggs. Ruth wondered why it tasted so good amid such primitive surroundings; yet everything was so clean and tidy, though coarse and plain. When they went to pay their bill the proprietor said their beds would be only twenty-five cents apiece because they had had no pillow. If they had had a pillow he would have had to charge them fifty cents. The food was fabulously cheap. They looked around and wondered how it could be done. It was obvious that no tips would be received, and that money was no consideration. In fact, the man told them his orders were merely to pay expenses. He gave them a parting word of good cheer, and promised to try and make them more comfortable if they wanted to return that night, and so they started out for camp. Ruth was silent and thoughtful. She was wishing she had had the boldness to ask this quaint Christian man some of the questions that troubled her. He looked as if he knew God, and she felt as if he might be able to make some things plain to her. But her life had been so hedged about by conventionalities that it seemed an impossible thing to her to open her lips on the subject to any living being—unless it might be to John Cameron. It was queer how they two had grown together in the last few months. Why could they not have known one another before?

Then there came a vision of what her aunt might have thought, and possible objections that might have come up if they had been intimate friends earlier. In fact, that, too, seemed practically to have been an impossibility. How had the war torn away the veil from foolish laws of social rank and station! Never again could she submit to much of the system that had been the foundation of her life so far. Somehow she must find a way to tear her spirit free from things that were not real. The thought of the social activities that would face her at home under the guise of patriotism turned her soul sick with loathing. When she went back home after he was gone she would find a way to do something real in the world that would make for righteousness and peace somehow. Knitting and dancing with lonesome soldiers did not satisfy her.

That was a wonderful day and they made the most of every hour, realizing that it would probably be the last day they had together for many a long month or year.

In the morning they stepped into the great auditorium and attended a Y.M.C.A. service for an hour, but their hearts were so full, and they all felt so keenly that this day was to be the real farewell, and they could not spare a moment of it, that presently they slipped away to the quiet of the woods once more, for it was hard to listen to the music and keep the tears back. Mrs. Cameron especially found it impossible to keep her composure.

Sunday afternoon she went into the Hostess' House to lie down in the rest room for a few minutes, and sent the two young people off for a walk by themselves.

Cameron took Ruth to the log in the woods and showed her his little Testament and the covenant he had signed. Then they opened their hearts together about the eternal things of life; shyly, at first, and then with the assurance that sympathy brings. Cameron told her that he was trying to find God, and Ruth told him about their experiences the night before. She also shyly promised that she would pray for him, although she had seldom until lately done very much real praying for herself.

It was a beautiful hour wherein they travelled miles in their friendship; an hour in which their souls came close while they sat on the log under the trees with long silences in the intervals of their talk.

It was whispered at the barracks that evening at five when Cameron went back for "Retreat" that this was the last night. They would move in the morning surely, perhaps before. He hurried back to the Hostess' House where he had left his guests to order the supper for all, feeling that he must make the most of every minute.

Passing the officers' headquarters he heard the raucous laugh of Wainwright, and caught a glimpse of his fat head and neck through a window. His heart sank! Wainwright was back! Then he had been sent for, and they must be going that night!

He fled to the Hostess' House and was silent and distraught as he ate his supper. Suppose Wainwright should come in while they were there and see Ruth and spoil those last few minutes together! The thought was unbearable.

Nobody wanted much supper and they wandered outside in the soft evening air. There was a hushed sorrow over everything. Even the roughest soldiers were not ashamed of tears. Little faded mothers clung to big burly sons, and their sons smoothed their gray hair awkwardly and were not ashamed. A pair of lovers sat at the foot of a tree hand in hand and no one looked at them, except in sympathy. There were partings everywhere. A few wives with little children in their arms were writing down hurried directions and receiving a bit of money; but most desolate of all was the row of lads lined up near the station whose friends were gone, or had not come at all, and who had to stand and endure the woe of others.

"Couldn't we *walk* out of camp?" asked Ruth suddenly. "Must we go on that awful trolley? Last night everybody was weeping. I wanted to weep, too. It is only a few steps from the end of camp to our quarters. Or is it too far for you, Mrs. Cameron?"

"Nothing is too far to-night so I may be with my boy one hour longer."

"Then we must start at once," said Cameron, "there is barely time to reach the outskirts before the hour when all visitors must be out of camp. It is over three miles, mother."

"I can walk it if Ruth can," said the mother smiling bravely.

He drew an arm of each within his own and started off, glad to be out of Wainwright's neighborhood, gladder still to have a little longer with those he loved.

Out through the deserted streets they passed, where empty barracks were being prepared for the next draft men; past the Tank Headquarters and the colored barracks, the storehouses and more barracks just emptied that afternoon into troop trains; out beyond the great laundry and on up the cinder road to the top of the hill and the end of the way.

There at last, in sight of the Military Police, pacing back and forth at the entrance to camp, with the twinkling lights of the village beyond, and the long wooded road winding back to camp, they paused to say good-bye. The cinder path and the woods at its edge made a blot of greenish black against a brilliant stormy sky. The sun was setting like a ball of fire behind the trees, and some strange freak of its rays formed a golden cross resting back against the clouds, its base buried among the woods, its cross bar rising brilliant against the black of a thunder cloud.

"Look!" said Ruth, "it is an omen!" They looked and a great wonder and awe came upon them. The Cross!

Cameron looked back and then down at her and smiled.

"It will lead you safely home," she said softly and laid her hand in his. He held her fingers close for an instant and his eyes dared some of the things his lips would never have spoken now even if they two had been alone.

The Military Police stepped up:

"You don't have to stay out here to say good-bye. You can come into the station right here and sit down. Or if your friends are going to the village you may go with them, Comrade. I can trust you to come back right away."

"I thank you!" Cameron said. "That is the kindest thing that has happened to me at this camp. I wish I could avail myself of it, but I have barely time to get back to the barracks within the hour given me. Perhaps—" and he glanced anxiously across the road toward the village. "Could you just keep an eye out that my ladies reach the Salvation Army Hut all right?"

"Sure!" said the big soldier heartily, "I'll go myself. I'm just going off duty and I'll see them safe to the door."

He stepped a little away and gave an order to his men, and so they said good-bye and watched Cameron go down the road into the sunset with the golden cross blazing above him as he walked lower and lower down the hill into the shadow of the dark woods and the thunder cloud. But brightly the cross shone above him as long as they could see, and just before he stepped into the darkness where the road turned he paused, waved his hat, and so passed on out of their sight.

15

THE first night on the water was one of unspeakable horror to Cameron. They had scarcely begun to feel the roll of the waves before Captain Wurtz manifested his true nature. At six o'clock and broad daylight, he ordered the men below, had them locked in, and all the port holes closed!

The place was packed, the heat was unbearable, the motion increasing all the time, and the air soon became intolerable. In vain the men protested, and begged for air. Their requests were all denied. The captain trusted no man. He treated them as if they were hounds. Wainwright stood by the captain's side, smoking the inevitable cigarette, his eyes narrowly watching Cameron, when the order was given; but no onlooker could have told from Cameron's well trained face whether he had heard or not. Well he knew where those orders had originated, and instantly he saw a series of like torments. Wainwright had things in his own hands for this voyage. Wurtz was his devoted slave. For Wainwright had money, and used it freely with his captain, and Wainwright well knew how to think up tortures. It was really the only thing in which he was clever. And here again was an instance of practice making perfect, for Wainwright had done little else since his kindergarten days than to think up trials for those who would not bow to his peevish will. He seemed to be gifted in finding out exactly what would be the finest kind of torture for any given soul who happened to be his victim. He had the mind of Nero and the spirit of a mean little beast. The wonder, the great miracle was, that he had not in some way discovered that Ruth had been visiting the camp, and taken his revenge before she left. This was the first thought that came to Cameron when he found himself shut into the murky atmosphere. The next thought was that perhaps he had discovered it and this was the result. He felt himself the Jonah for the company, and as the dreadful hours went by would fain have cast himself into the sea if there had been a possible way of escape.

It was not an American transport on which they were sailing, and the captain was not responsible for the food, but he might have refused to allow such meals to be served to his men if he had cared. He did not care, that was the whole trouble. He ate and drank, principally drank, and did whatever Wainwright suggested. When a protest came up to him he turned it down with a laugh, and said: "Oh, that's good enough for a buck private," and went on with his dirty jokes.

The supper that first night was abominable, some unpleasant kind of meat cooked with cabbage, and though they tried to eat it, many of them could not keep it down. The ship rolled and the men grew sick. The atmosphere became fetid. Each moment seemed more impossible than the last. There was no room to move, neither could one get out and away. After supper the men lay down in the only place there was to lie, two men on the tables, two men on the benches each side, two men on the floor between, and so on all over the cabin, packed like eggs in a box.

They sent a message to their captain begging for air, but he only laughed, and sent word back they would have air enough before they got through with this war.

The night wore on and Cameron lay on his scant piece of floor—he had given his bench to a sicker man than himself—and tried to sleep. But sleep did not visit his eyelids. He was thinking, thinking. "I'm going to find God! I'm going to search for Him with all my heart, and somehow I'm going to find Him before I'm done. I may never come home, but I'll find God, anyhow! It's the only thing that makes life bearable!"

Then would come a wave of hate for his enemy and wipe out all other thoughts, and he would wrestle in his heart with the desire to kill Wainwright—yes, and the captain, too. As some poor wretch near him would writhe and groan in agony his rage would boil up anew, his fists would clench, and he would half rise to go to the door and overpower that guard! If only he could get up to where the officers were enjoying themselves! Oh, to bring them down here and bind them in this loathsome atmosphere, feed them with this food, stifle them in the dark with closed port holes! His brain was fertile with thoughts of revenge. Then suddenly across his memory would flash the words: "If with all your heart ye seek Him," and he would reach out in longing: Oh, if he could find God, surely God would stop a thing like this! Did God have no power in His own earth?

Slowly, painfully, the days dragged by, each worse than the last. In the mornings the men must go on deck whether they were sick or not, and must stay there all day, no matter what the weather. If they were wet they must dry out by the heat of their bodies. There was no possibility of getting at their kit bags, it was so crowded.

No man was allowed to open one. All they had was the little they carried in their packs. How they lived through it was a wonder, but live they did. Perhaps the worst torture of all was the great round cork life preserver in the form of a cushioned ring which they were obliged to wear night and day. A man could never lie down comfortably with it on, and if from sheer exhaustion he fell asleep he awoke with his back aching tortures. The meat and cabbage was varied twice by steamed fish served in its scales, tails, fins, heads, and entrails complete. All that they got which was really eatable was a small bun served in the morning, and boiled potatoes occasionally.

Nevertheless, these hardships would have been as nothing to Cameron if they had not represented to him hate, pure and simple. He felt, and perhaps justly, that if Wainwright had not wished to make him suffer, these things would surely have been mitigated.

The day came at last when they stood on the deck and watched the strange foreign shore draw nearer. Cameron, stern and silent, stood apart from the rest. For the moment his anger toward Wainwright was forgotten, though he could hear the swaggering tones from the deck above, and the noisome laughter of Wurtz in response. Cameron was looking into the face of the future, wondering what it would mean for him. Out there was the strange country. What did it hold for him? Was God there? How he wanted God to go with him and help him face the future!

There was much delay in landing, and getting ready to move. The men were weak from sickness and long fasting. They tottered as they stood, but they had to stand—unless they dropped. They turned wan faces toward one another and tried to smile. Their fine American pep was gone, hopelessly, yet they grinned feebly now and then and got off a weak little joke or two. For the most part they glared when the officers came by—especially two—those two. The wrath toward them had been brewing long and deep as each man lay weltering through those unbearable nights. Hardship they could bear, and pain, and sickness—but tyranny *never*!

Someone had written a letter. It was not the first. There had been others on ship board protesting against their treatment. But this letter was a warning to that captain and lieutenant. If they ever led these men into battle *they* would be killed before the battle began. It was signed by the company. It had been a unanimous vote. Now as they stood staring leadenly at the strange sights about them, listening to the new jargon of the shore, noting the quaint headdresses and wooden sabots of the people with a fine scorn of indifference, they thought of that letter in hard phrases of rage. And bitterest of all were the thoughts of John Cameron as he stood in his place awaiting orders.

They were hungry, these men, and unfit, when at last the order came to march, and they had to hike it straight up a hill with a great pack on their backs. It was not that they minded the packs or the hike or the hunger. It was the injustice of their treatment that weighed upon them like a burden that human nature could not bear. They had come to lift such a burden from the backs of another nation, and they had been treated like dogs all the way over! Like the low rumbling of oncoming thunder was the blackness of their countenances as they marched up, up, and up into Brest. The sun grew hot, and their knees wobbled under them from sheer weakness; strong men when they started, who were fine and fit, now faint like babies, yet with spirits unbroken, and great vengeance in their hearts. They would fight, oh they would fight, yes, but they would see that captain out of the way first! Here and there by the way some fell—the wonder is they all did not—and had to be picked up by the ambulances; and at last they had to be ordered to stop and rest! They! Who had come over here to flaunt their young strength in the face of the enemy! *They* to fall *before the fight was begun.* This, too, they laid up against their tyrant.

But there was welcome for them, nevertheless. Flowers and wreaths and bands of music met them as they went through the town, and women and little children flung them kisses and threw blossoms in their way. This revived somewhat the drooping spirits with which they had gone forth, and when they reached camp and got a decent meal they felt better, and more reasonable. Still the bitterness was there, against those two who had used their power unworthily. That night, lying on a hard little cot in camp Cameron tried to pray, his heart full of longing for God, yet found the heavens as brass, and could not find words to cry out, except in bitterness. Somehow he did not feel he was getting on at all in his search, and from sheer weariness and discouragement he fell asleep at last.

Three days and nights of rest they had and then were packed into tiny freight cars with a space so small that they had to take turns sitting down. Men had to sleep sitting or standing, or wherever they could find space to lie down. So they started across France, three days and awful nights they went, weary and sore and bitter still. But they had air and they were better fed. Now and then they could stand up and look out through a crack. Once in a while a fellow could get space to stretch out for a few minutes. Cameron awoke once and found feet all over him, feet even in his face. Yet these things were what he had expected. He did not whine. He was toughened for such experiences, so were the men about him. The hardness merely brought out their courage.

They were getting their spirits back now as they neared the real scene of action. The old excitement and call to action were creeping back into their blood. Now and then a song would pipe out, or a much abused banjo or mandolin would twang and bring forth their voices. It was only when an officer walked by or mention would be made of the captain or lieutenant that their looks grew black again and they fell silent. Injustice and tyranny, the things they had come out to fight, that they would not forgive nor forget. Their spirits were reviving but their hate was there.

At last they detrained and marched into a little town. This was France!

Cameron looked about him in dismay. A scramble of houses and barns, sort of two-in-one affairs. Where was the beauty of France about which he had read so often? Mud was everywhere. The streets were deep with it, the ground was sodden, rain-soaked. It was raining even then. Sunny France!

It was in a barnyard deep in manure where Cameron's tent was set up. Little brown tents set close together, their flies dovetailing so that more could be put in a given space.

Dog weary he strode over the stakes that held them, and looked upon the place where he was to sleep. Its floor was almost a foot deep in water! Rank, ill smelling water! Pah! Was this intention that he should have been billeted here? Some of the men had dry places. Of course, it might have just happened, but—well, what was the use. Here he must sleep for he could not stand up any longer or he would fall over. So he heaped up a pillow of the muck, spread his blanket out and lay down. At least his head would be high enough out of the water so that he would not drown in his sleep, and with his feet in water, and the cold ooze creeping slowly through his heavy garments, he dropped immediately into oblivion. There were no prayers that night. His heart was full of hate. The barnyard was in front of an old stone farm house, and in that farm house were billeted the captain and his favorite first lieutenant. Cameron could hear his raucous laugh and the clinking of the wine glasses, almost the gurgle of the wine. The thought of Wainwright was his last conscious one before he slept. Was it of intention that he should have been put here close by, where Wainwright could watch his every move?

As the days went by and real training began, with French officers working them hard until they were ready to drop at night, gradually Cameron grew stolid. It seemed sometimes as if he had always been here, splashing along in the mud, soaked with rain, sleeping in muck at night, never quite dry, never free from cold and discomfort, never quite clean, always training, the boom of the battle afar, but never getting there. Where was the front? Why didn't they get there and fight and get done with it all?

The rain poured down, day after day. Ammunition trains rolled by. More men marched in, more marched on, still they trained. It seemed eons since he had bade Ruth and his mother good-bye that night at the camp. No mail had come. Oh, if he could just hear a word from home! If he only had her picture! They had taken some together at camp and she had promised to have them developed and send them, but they would probably never reach him. And it were better if they did not. Wainwright was censor. If he recognized the writing nothing would ever reach him he was sure. Still, Wainwright had nothing to do with the incoming mail, only the outgoing. Well, Wainwright should never censor his letters. He would find a way to get letters out that

Wainwright had never censored, or he would never send any.

But the days dragged by in rain and mud and discouragement, and no letters came. Once or twice he attempted to write a respectable letter to his mother, but he felt so hampered with the thought of Wainwright having to see it that he kept it securely in his pocket, and contented himself with gay-pictured postcards which he had purchased in Brest, on which he inscribed a few non-committal sentences, always reminding them of the censor, and his inability to say what he would, and always ending, "Remember me to my friend, and tell her I have forgotten nothing but cannot write at present for reasons which I cannot explain."

At night he lay on his watery couch and composed long letters to Ruth which he dared not put on paper lest somehow they should come into the hands of Wainwright. He took great satisfaction in the fact that he had succeeded in slipping through a post card addressed to herself from Brest, through the kindness and understanding of a small boy who agreed to mail it in exchange for a package of chewing gum. Here at the camp there was no such opportunity, but he would wait and watch for another chance. Meantime the long separation of miles, and the creeping days, gave him a feeling of desolation such as he had never experienced before. He began to grow introspective. He fancied that perhaps he had overestimated Ruth's friendship for him. The dear memories he had cherished during the voyage were brought out in the nightwatches and ruthlessly reviewed, until his own shy hope that the light in her eyes had been for him began to fade, and in its place there grew a conviction that happiness of earth was never for him. For, he reasoned, if she cared, why did she not write? At least a post card? Other fellows were getting letters now and then. Day after day he waited when the mail was distributed, but nothing ever came. His mother seemed to have forgotten, too. Surely, all these weeks, some word would have come through. It was not in reason that his mail should be delayed beyond others. Could it be that there was false play somehow? Was Wainwright at the bottom of this? Or had something happened to his mother, and had Ruth forgotten?

THE weeks rolled by. The drilling went on. At last word came that the company was to move up farther toward the front. They prepared for a long hike almost eagerly, not knowing yet what was before them. Anything was better than this intolerable waiting.

Solemnly under a leaden sky they gathered; sullenly went through their inspection; stolidly, dully, they marched away through the rain and mud and desolation. The nights were cold and their clothes seemed thin and inadequate. They had not been paid since they came over, so there was no chance to buy any little comfort, even if it had been for sale. A longing for sweets and home puddings and pies haunted their waking hours as they trudged wearily hour after hour, kilometer after kilometer, coming ever nearer, nearer.

For two days they hiked, and then entrained for a long uncomfortable night, and all the time Cameron's soul was crying out within him for the living God. In these days he read much in the little Testament whenever there was a rest by the wayside, and he could draw apart from the others. Ever his soul grew hungrier as he neared the front, and knew his time now was short. There were days when he had the feeling that he must stop tramping and do something about this great matter that hung over him, and then Wainwright would pass by and cast a sharp direction at him with a sneer in the curl of his moustache, and all the fury of his being would rise up, until he would clench his fists in helpless wrath, as Wainwright swaggered on. To think how easily he could drag him in the dust if it only came to a fair fight between them! But Wainwright had all the advantage now, with such a captain on his side!

That night ride was a terrible experience. Cameron, with his thoughts surging and pounding through his brain, was in no condition to come out of hardships fresh and fit. He was overcome with weariness when he climbed into the box car with thirty-nine other fellows just as weary, just as discouraged, just as homesick.

There was only room for about twenty to travel comfortably in that car, but they cheerfully huddled together and took their turns sitting down, and somewhere along in the night it came Cameron's turn to slide down on the floor and stretch out for a while; or perhaps his utter weariness made him drop there involuntarily, because he could no longer keep awake. For a few minutes the delicious ache of lying flat enveloped him and carried him away into unconsciousness with a lulling ecstasy. Then suddenly Wainwright seemed to loom over him and demand that he rise and let him lie down in his place. It seemed to Cameron that the lethargy that had stolen over him as he fell asleep was like heavy bags of sand tied to his hands and feet. He could not rise if he would. He thought he tried to tell Wainwright that he was unfair. He was an officer and had better accommodations. What need had he to come back here and steal a weary private's sleep. But his lips refused to open and his throat gave out no sound. Wainwright seemed gradually stooping nearer, nearer, with a large soft hand about his throat, and his little pig eyes gleaming like two points of green light, his selfish mouth all pursed up as it used to be when the fellows stole his all-day-sucker, and held it tantalizingly above his reach. One of his large cushiony knees was upon Cameron's chest now, and the breath was going from him. He gasped, and tried to shout to the other fellows that this was the time to do away with this tyrant, this captain's pet, but still only a croak would come from his lips. With one mighty effort he wrenched his hands and feet into action, and lunged up at the mighty bully above him, struggling, clutching wildly for his throat, with but one thought in his dreaming brain, to kill—to kill! Sound came to his throat at last, action to his sleeping body, and struggling himself loose from the two comrades who had fallen asleep upon him and almost succeeded in smothering him, he gave a hoarse yell and got to his feet.

They cursed and laughed at him, and snuggled down good naturedly to their broken slumbers again, but Cameron stood in his corner, glaring out the tiny crack into the dark starless night that was whirling by, startled into thoughtfulness. The dream had been so vivid that he could not easily get rid of it. His heart was boiling hot with rage at his old enemy, yet something stronger was there, too, a great horror at himself. He had been about to kill a fellow creature! To what pass had he come!

And somewhere out in that black wet night, a sweet white face gleamed, with brown hair blown about it, and the mist of the storm in its locks. It was as if her spirit had followed him and been present in that dream to shame him. Supposing the dream had been true, and he had actually killed Wainwright! For he knew by the wild beating of his heart, by the hotness of his wrath as he came awake, that nothing would have stayed his hand if he had been placed in such a situation.

It was *like* a dream to hover over a poor worn tempest-tossed soul in that way and make itself verity; demand that he should live it out again and again and face the future that would have followed such a set of circumstances. He had to see Ruth's sad, stern face, the sorrowful eyes full of tears, the reproach, the disappointment, the alien lifting of her chin. He knew her so well; could so easily conjecture what her whole attitude would be, he thought. And then he must needs go on to think out once more just what relation there might be between his enemy and the girl he loved—think it out more carefully than he had ever let himself do before. All he knew about the two, how their home grounds adjoined, how their social set and standing and wealth was the same, how they had often been seen together; how Wainwright had boasted!

All night he stood and thought it out, glowering between the cracks of the car at the passing whirl, differentiating through the blackness now and then a group of trees or buildings or a quick flash of furtive light, but mainly darkness and monotony. It was if he were tied to the tail of a comet that dashed hellwards for a billion years, so long the night extended till the dull gray dawn. There was no God anywhere in that dark night. He had forgotten about Him entirely. He was perhaps strongly conscious of the devil at his right hand.

They detrained and hiked across a bit of wet country that was all alike—all mud, in the dull light that grew only to accentuate the ugliness and dreariness of everything. Sunny France! And this was sunny France!

At last they halted along a muddy roadside and lined up for what seemed an interminable age, waiting for something, no one knew what, nor cared. They were beyond caring, most of them, poor boys! If their mothers had appeared with a bowl of bread and milk and called them to bed they would have wept in her arms with joy. They stood apathetically and waited, knowing that sometime after another interminable age had passed, the red tape necessary to move a large body like themselves would be unwound, and everything go on again to another dreary halt somewhere. Would it ever be over? The long, long trail?

Cameron stood with the rest in a daze of discouragement, not taking the trouble to think any more. His head was hot and his chest felt heavy, reminding him of Wainwright's fat knee; and he had an ugly cough.

Suddenly someone—a comrade—touched him on the shoulder.

"Come on in here, Cammie, you're all in. This is the Salvation Army Hut!"

Cameron turned. Salvation Army! It sounded like the bells of heaven. Ah! It was something he could think back to, that little Salvation Army Hut at camp! It brought the tears into his throat in a great lump. He lurched after his friend, and dropped into the chair where he was pushed, sliding his arms out on the table before him and dropping his head quickly to hide his emotion. He couldn't think what was the matter with him. He seemed to be all giving way.

"He's all in!" he heard the voice of his friend, "I thought maybe you could do something for him. He's a good old sport!"

Then a gentle hand touched his shoulder, lightly, like his mother's hand. It thrilled him and he lifted his bleared eyes and looked into the face of a kindly gray-haired woman.

She was not a handsome woman, though none of the boys would ever let her be called homely, for they claimed her smile was so glorious that it gave her precedence in beauty to the greatest belle on earth. There was a real mother lovelight in her eyes now when she looked at Cameron, and she held a cup of steaming hot coffee in her hand, real coffee with sugar and cream and a rich aroma that gave life to his sinking soul.

"Here, son, drink this!" she said, holding the cup to his lips.

He opened his lips eagerly and then remembered and drew back:

"No," he said, drawing away, "I forgot, I haven't any money. We're all dead broke!" He tried to pull himself together and look like a man.

But the coffee cup came close to his lips again and the rough motherly hand stole about his shoulders to support him:

"That's all right!" she said in a low, matter-of-fact tone. "You don't need money here, son, you've got home, and I'm your mother to-night. Just drink this and then come in there behind those boxes and lie down on my bed and get a wink of sleep. You'll be yourself again in a little while. That's it, son! You've hiked a long way. Now forget it and take comfort."

So she soothed him till he surely must be dreaming again, and wondered which was real, or if perhaps he had a fever and hallucinations. He reached a furtive hand and felt of the pine table, and the chair on which he sat to make sure that he was awake, and then he looked into her kind gray eyes and smiled.

She led him into the little improvised room behind the counter and tucked him up on her cot with a big warm blanket.

"That's all right now, son," she whispered, "don't you stir till you feel like it. I'll look after you and your friend will let you know if there is any call for you. Just you rest."

He thanked her with his eyes, too weary to speak a word, and so he dropped into a blessed sleep.

When he awakened slowly to consciousness again there was a smell in the air of more coffee, delicious coffee. He wondered if it was the same cup, and this only another brief phase of his own peculiar state. Perhaps he had not been asleep at all, but had only closed his eyes and opened them again. But no, it was night, and there were candles lit beyond the barricade of boxes. He could see their flicker through the cracks, and shadows were falling here and there grotesquely on the bit of canvas that formed another wall. There was some other odor on the air, too. He sniffed delightedly like a little child, something sweet and alluring, reminding one of the days when mother took the gingerbread and pies out of the oven. No—doughnuts, that was it! Doughnuts! Not doughnuts just behind the trenches! How could that be?

He stirred and raised up on one elbow to look about him.

There were two other cots in the room, arranged neatly with folded blankets. A box in between held a few simple toilet articles, a tin basin and a bucket of water. He eyed them greedily. When had he had a good wash. What luxury!

He dropped back on the cot and all at once became aware that there were strange sounds in the air above the building in which he lay, strange and deep, yet regular and with a certain booming monotony as if they had been going on a long time, and he had been too preoccupied to take notice of them. A queer frenzy seized his heart. This, then, was the sound of battle in the distance! He was here at the front at last! And that was the sound of enemy shells! How strange it seemed! How it gripped the soul with the audacity of it all! How terrible, and yet how exciting to be here at last! And yet he had an unready feeling. Something was still undone to prepare him for this ordeal. It was his subconscious self that was crying out for God. His material self had sensed the doughnuts that were frying so near to him, and he looked up eagerly to welcome whoever was coming tiptoeing in to see if he was awake, with a nice hot plate of them for him to eat!

He swung to a sitting posture, and received them and the cup of hot chocolate that accompanied them with eagerness, like a little child whose mother had promised them if he would be good. Strange how easy and natural it was to fall into the ways of this gracious household. Would one call it that? It seemed so like a home!

While he was eating, his buddy slipped in smiling excitedly:

"Great news, Cammie! We've got a new captain! And, oh boy! He's a peach! He sat on our louie first off! You oughtta have seen poor old Wainwright's face when he shut him up at the headquarters. Boy, you'd a croaked! It was rich!"

Cameron finished the last precious bite of his third hot doughnut with a gulp of joy:

"What's become of Wurtz?" he asked anxiously.

"Canned, I guess," hazarded the private. "I did hear they took him to a sanitarium, nervous breakdown, they said. I'll tell the world he'd have had one for fair if he'd stayed with this outfit much longer. I only wish they'd have taken his little pet along with him. This is no place for little Harold and he'll find it out now he's got a real captain. Good-night! How d'you 'spose he ever got his commission, anyway? Well, how are you, old top? Feelin' better? I knew they'd fix you up here. They're reg'ler guys! Well, I guess we better hit the hay. Come on, I'll show you where your billet is. I looked out for a place with a good water-tight roof. What d'ye think of the orchestra Jerry is playing out there on the front? Some noise, eh, what? Say, this little old hut is some good place to tie up to, eh, pard! I've seen 'em before, that's how I knew."

During the days that followed Cameron spent most of his leisure time in the Salvation Army Hut.

He did not hover around the victrola as he would probably have done several months before, nor yet often join his voice in the ragtime song that was almost continuous at the piano, regardless of near-by shells, and usually accompanied by another tune on the victrola. He did not hover around the cooks and seek to make himself needful to them there, placing himself at the seat of supplies and handy when he was hungry—as did many. He sat at one of the far tables, often writing letters or reading his little book, or more often looking off into space, seeing those last days at camp, and the faces of his mother and Ruth.

There was more than one reason why he spent much of his time here. The hut was not frequented much by officers, although they did come sometimes, and were always welcomed, but never deferred to. Wainwright would not be likely to be about and it was always a relief to feel free from the presence of his enemy. But gradually a third reason came to play a prominent part in bringing him here, and that was the atmosphere. He somehow felt as if he were among real people who were living life earnestly, as if the present were not all there was.

There came a day when they were to move on up to the actual front. Cameron wrote letters, such as he had not dared to write before, for he had found out that these women could get them to his people in case anything should happen to him, and so he left a little letter for

Ruth and one for his mother, and asked the woman with the gray eyes to get them back home somehow.

There was not much of moment in the letters. Even thus he dared not speak his heart for the iron of Wainwright's poison had entered into his soul. He had begun to think that perhaps, in spite of all her friendliness, Ruth really belonged to another world, not his world. Yet just her friendliness meant much to him in his great straight of loneliness. He would take that much of her, at least, even if it could never be more. He would leave a last word for her. If behind his written words there was breaking heart and tender love, she would never dream it. If his soul was really taking another farewell of her, what harm, since he said no sad word. Yet it did him good to write these letters and feel a reasonable assurance that they would sometime reach their destination.

There was a meeting held that night in the hut. He had never happened to attend one before, although he had heard the boys say they enjoyed them. One of his comrades asked him to stay, and a quick glance told him the fellow needed him, had chosen him for moral support.

So Cameron sat in a shadowy corner of the crowded room, and listened to the singing, wild and strong, and with no hint of coming battle in its full rolling lilt. He noted with satisfaction how the "Long, Long Trail," and "Pack Up Your Troubles in Your Old Kit Bag" gradually gave place to "Tell Mother I'll Be There," and "When the Roll is Called Up Yonder," growing strong and full and solemn in the grand old melody of "Abide With Me." There were fellows there who but a few hours before had been shooting crap, whose lips had been loud with cheerful curses. Now they sat and sang with all their hearts, the heartiest of the lot. It was a curious psychological study to watch them. Some of them were just as keen now on the religious side of their natures as they had been with their sport or their curses. Theirs were primitive natures, easily wrought upon by the atmosphere of the moment, easily impressed by the solemnity of the hour, nearer, perhaps, to stopping to think about God and eternity than ever before in their lives. But there were also others here, thoughtful fellows who were strong and brave, who had done their duty and borne their hardships with the best, yet whose faces now were solemn with earnestness, to whom this meeting meant a last sacrament before they passed to meet their test. Cameron felt his heart in perfect sympathy with the gathering, and when the singing stopped for a few minutes, and the clear voice of a young girl began to pray, he bowed his head with a smart of tears in his eyes. She was a girl who had just arrived that day, and she reminded him of Ruth. She had pansy-blue eyes and long gold ripples in her abundant hair. It soothed him like a gentle hand on his heart to hear her speak those words of prayer to God, praying for them all as if they were her own brothers, praying as if she understood just how they felt this night before they went on their way. She was so young and gently cared for, this girl with her plain soldier's uniform, and her fearlessness, praying as composedly out there under fire as if she trusted perfectly that her heavenly Father had control of everything and would do the best for them all. What a wonderful girl! Or, no—was it perhaps a wonderful trust? Stay, was it not perhaps a wonderful heavenly Father? And she had found Him? Perhaps she could tell him the way and how he had missed it in his search!

With this thought in his mind he lingered as the most of the rest passed out, and turning he noticed that the man who had come with him lingered also, and edged up to the front where the lassie stood talking with a group of men.

Then one of the group spoke up boldly:

"Say, Cap," he addressed her almost reverently, as if he had called her some queenly name instead of captain, "say, Cap, I want to ask you a question. Some of those fellows that preached to us have been telling us that if we go over there, and don't come back it'll be all right with us, just because we died fighting for liberty. But we don't believe that dope. Why—d'ye mean to tell me, Cap, that if a fellow has been rotten all his life he gets saved just because he happened to get shot in a battle? Why some of us didn't even come over here to fight because we wanted to; we have to, we were drafted. Do you mean to tell me that makes it all right over here? I can't see that at all. And we want to know the truth. You dope it out for us, Cap."

The young captain lassie slowly shook her head:

"No, just dying doesn't save you, son." There was a note of tenderness in that "son" as those Salvation Army lassies spoke it, that put them infinitely above the common young girl, as if some angelic touch had set them apart for their holy ministry. It was as if God were using their lips and eyes and spirits to speak to these, his children, in their trying hour.

"You see, it's this way. Everybody has sinned, and the penalty of sin is death. You all know that?"

Her eyes searched their faces, and appealed to the truth hidden in the depths of their souls. They nodded, those boys who were going out soon to face death. They were willing to tell her that they acknowledged their sins. They did not mind if they said it before each other. They meant it now. Yes, they were sinners and it was because they knew they were that they wanted to know what chances they stood in the other world.

"But God loved us all so much that He wanted to make a way for us to escape the punishment," went on the sweet steady voice, seeming to bring the very love of the Father down into their midst with its forceful, convincing tone. "And so He sent His son, Jesus Christ, to take our place and die on the Cross in our stead. Whoever is willing to accept His atonement may be saved. And it's all up to us whether we will take it or not. It isn't anything we can do or be. It is just taking Jesus as our Saviour, believing in Him, and taking Him at His word."

Cameron lingered and knelt with the rest when she prayed again for them, and in his own heart he echoed the prayer of acceptance that others were putting up. As he went out into the black night, and later, on the silent march through the dark, he was turning it over in his mind. It seemed to him the simplest, the most sensible explanation of the plan of Salvation he had ever heard. He wondered if the minister at home knew all this and had meant it when he tried to explain. But no, that minister had not tried to explain, he had told him he would grow into it, and here he was perhaps almost at the end and he had not grown into it yet. That young girl to-night had said it took only an instant to settle the whole thing, and she looked as if her soul was resting on it. Why could he not get peace? Why could he not find God?

Then out of the dark and into his thoughts came a curse and a sneer and a curt rebuke from Wainwright, and all his holy and beautiful thoughts fled! He longed to lunge out of the dark and spring upon that fat, flabby lieutenant, and throttle him. So, in bitterness of spirit he marched out to face the foe.

17

WHEN Ruth Macdonald got back from camp she found herself utterly dissatisfied with her old life. The girls in her social set were full of war plans. They had one and all enlisted in every activity that was going. Each one appeared in some pretty and appropriate uniform, and took the new regime with as much eagerness and enthusiasm as ever she had put into dancing and dressing.

Not that they had given up either of those employments. Oh, dear no! When they were not busy getting up little dances for the poor dear soldier boys from the nearby camps, they were learning new solo steps wherewith to entertain those soldier boys when their turn came to go to camp and keep up the continuous performance that seemed to be necessary to the cheering of a good soldier. And as for dressing, no one need ever suggest again a uniform for women as the solution of the high cost of dressing. The number of dainty devices of gold braid and red stars and silver tassels that those same staid uniforms developed made plain forever that the woman who chooses can make even a uniform distinctive and striking and altogether costly. In short they went into the war with the same superficial flightiness formerly employed in the social realms. They went dashing here and there in their high-power cars on solemn errands, with all the nonchalance of their ignorance and youth, till one, knowing some of them well, trembled for the errand if it were important. And many of them were really useful, which only goes to prove that a tremendous amount of unsuspected power is wasted every year and that unskilled labor often accomplishes almost as much as skilled. Some of them secured positions in the Navy Yard, or in other public offices, where they were thrown delightfully into intimacies with officers, and were able to step over the conventionalities of their own social positions into wildly exciting Bohemian adventures under the popular guise of patriotism, without a rebuke from their elders. There was not a dull hour in the little town. The young men of their social set might all be gone to war, but there were others, and the whirl of life went on gaily for the thoughtless butterflies, who danced and knitted and drove motor cars, and made bandages and just rejoiced to walk the streets knitting on the Sabbath day, a gay cretonne knitting bag on arm, and knitting needles plying industriously as if the world would go naked if they did not work every minute. Just a horde of rebellious young creatures, who at heart enjoyed the unwonted privilege of breaking the Sabbath and shocking a few fanatics, far more than they really cared to knit. But nobody had time to pry into the quality of such patriotism. There were too many other people doing the same thing, and so it passed everywhere for the real thing, and the world whirled on and tried to be gay to cover its deep heartache and stricken horror over the sacrifice of its sons.

But Ruth, although she bravely tried for several weeks, could not throw herself into such things. She felt that they were only superficial. There might be a moiety of good in all these things, but they were not the real big things of life; not the ways in which the vital help could be given, and she longed with her whole soul to get in on it somewhere.

The first Sabbath after her return from camp she happened into a bit of work which while it was in no way connected with war work, still helped to interest her deeply and keep her thinking along the lines that had been started while she was with John Cameron.

A quiet, shy, plain little woman, an old member of the church and noted for good work, came hurrying down the aisle after the morning service and implored a young girl in the pew just in front of Ruth to help her that afternoon in an Italian Sunday school she was conducting in a small settlement about a mile and a half from Bryne Haven:

"It's only to play the hymns, Miss Emily," she said. "Carrie Wayne has to go to a funeral. She always plays for me. I wouldn't ask you if I could play the least mite myself, but I can't. And the singing won't go at all without someone to play the piano."

"Oh, I'm sorry, Mrs. Beck, but I really can't!" pleaded Miss Emily quickly. "I promised to help out in the canteen work this afternoon. You know the troop trains are coming through, and Mrs. Martin wanted me to take her place all the afternoon."

Mrs. Beck's face expressed dismay. She gave a hasty glance around the rapidly emptying church.

"Oh, dear, I don't know what I'll do!" she said.

"Oh, let them do without singing for once," suggested the carefree Emily. "Everybody ought to learn to do without something in war time. We conserve sugar and flour, let the Italians conserve singing!" and with a laugh at her own brightness she hurried away.

Ruth reached forward and touched the troubled little missionary on the arm:

"Would I do?" she asked. "I never played hymns much, but I could try."

"Oh! Would you?" A flood of relief went over the woman's face, and Ruth was instantly glad she had offered. She took Mrs. Beck down to the settlement in her little runabout, and the afternoon's experience opened a new world to her. It was the first time she had ever come in contact with the really poor and lowly of the earth, and she proved herself a true child of God in that she did not shrink from them because many of them were dirty and poorly clad. Before the first afternoon was over she had one baby in her arms and three others hanging about her chair with adoring glances. They could not talk in her language, but they stared into her beautiful face with their great dark eyes, and spoke queer unintelligible words to one another about her. The whole little company were delighted with the new "pretty lady" who had come among them. They openly examined her simple lovely frock and hat and touched with shy furtive fingers the blue ribbon that floated over the bench from her girdle. Mrs. Beck was in the seventh heaven and begged her to come again, and Ruth, equally charmed, promised to go every Sunday. For it appeared that the wayward pianist was very irregular and had to be constantly coaxed.

Ruth entered into the work with zest. She took the children's class which formerly had been with the older ones, and gathering them about her told them Bible stories till their young eyes bulged with wonder and their little hearts almost burst with love of her. Love God? Of course they would. Try to please Jesus? Certainly, if "Mrs. Ruth," as they called her, said they should. They adored her.

She fell into the habit of going down during the week and slipping into their homes with a big basket of bright flowers from her home garden which she distributed to young and old. Even the men, when they happened to be home from work, wanted the flowers, and touched them with eager reverence. Somehow the little community of people so different from herself filled her thoughts more and more. She began to be troubled that some of the men drank and beat their wives and little children in consequence. She set herself to devise ways to keep them from it. She scraped acquaintance with one or two of the older boys in her own church and enlisted them to help her, and bought a moving picture machine which she took to the settlement. She spent hours attending moving picture shows that she might find the right films for their use. Fortunately she had money enough for all her schemes, and no one to hinder her good work, although Aunt Rhoda did object strenuously at first on the ground that she might "catch something." But Ruth only smiled and said: "That's just what I'm out for, Auntie, dear! I want to catch them all, and try to make them live better lives. Other people are going to France. I haven't got a chance to go yet, but while I stay here I must do something. I can't be an idler."

Aunt Rhoda looked at her quizzically. She wondered if Ruth was worried about one of her men friends—and which one?

"If you'd only take up some nice work for the Government, dear, such as the other girls are doing!" she sighed, "work that would bring you into contact with nice people! You always have to do something queer. I'm sure I don't know where you got your low tendencies!"

But Ruth would be off before more could be said.

This was an old topic of Aunt Rhoda's and had been most fully discussed during the young years of Ruth's life, so that she did not care to enter into it further.

But Ruth was not fully satisfied with just helping her Italians. The very week she came back from camp she had gone to their old family physician who held a high and responsible position in the medical world, and made her plea:

"Daddy-Doctor," she said, using her old childish name for him, "you've got to find a way for me to go over there and help the war. I know I don't know much about nursing, but I'm sure I could learn. I've taken care of Grandpa and Auntie a great many times and watched the trained nurses, and I'm sure if Lalla Farrington and Bernice Brooks could get into the Red Cross and go over in such a short time I'm as bright as they."

"Brighter!" said the old doctor eyeing her approvingly. "But what will your people say?"

"They'll have to let me, Daddy-Doctor. Besides, everybody else is doing it, and you know that has great weight with Aunt Rhoda."

"It's a hard life, child! You never saw much of pain and suffering and horror."

"Well, it's time, then."

"But those men over there you would have to care for will not be like your grandfather and aunt. They will be dirty and bloody, and covered with filth and vermin."

"Well, what of that!"

"Could you stand it?"

"So you think I'm a butterfly, too, do you, Daddy-Doctor? Well, I want to prove to you that I'm not. I've been doing my best to get used to dirt and distress. I washed a little sick Italian baby yesterday and helped it's mother scrub her floor and make the house clean."

"The dickens you did!" beamed the doctor proudly.

"I always knew you had a lot of grit. I guess you've got the right stuff in you. But say, if I help you you've got to tell me the real reason why you want to go, or else—nothing doing! Understand? I know you aren't like the rest, just wanting to get into the excitement and meet a lot of officers and have a good time so you can say afterward you were there. You aren't that kind of a girl. What's the real reason you want to go? Have you got somebody over there you're interested in?"

He looked at her keenly, with loving, anxious eyes as her father's friend who had known her from birth might look.

Ruth's face grew rosy, and her eyes dropped, but lifted again undaunted:

"And if I have, Daddy-Doctor, is there anything wrong about that?"

The doctor frowned:

"It isn't that fat chump of a Wainwright, is it? Because if it is I shan't lift my finger to help you go."

But Ruth's laugh rang out clear and free.

"Never! dear friend, never! Set your mind at rest about him," she finished, sobering down. "And if I care for someone, Daddy-Doctor, can't you trust me I'd pick out someone who was all right?"

"I suppose so!" grumbled the doctor only half satisfied, "but girls are so dreadfully blind."

"I think you'd like him," she hazarded, her cheeks growing pinker, "that is, you would if there *is* anybody," she corrected herself laughing. "But you see, it's a secret yet and maybe always will be. I'm not sure that he knows, and I'm not quite sure I know myself—"

"Oh, I see!" said the doctor watching her sweet face with a tender jealousy in his eyes. "Well, I suppose I'll help you to go, but I'll shoot him, remember, if he doesn't turn out to be all right. It would take a mighty superior person to be good enough for you, little girl."

"That's just what he is," said Ruth sweetly, and then rising and stooping over him she dropped a kiss on the wavy silver lock of hair that hung over the doctor's forehead.

"Thank you, Daddy-Doctor! I knew you would," she said happily. "And please don't be too long about it. I'm in a great hurry."

The doctor promised, of course. No one could resist Ruth when she was like that, and in due time certain forces were set in operation to the end that she might have her desire.

Meanwhile, as she waited, Ruth filled her days with thoughts of others, not forgetting Cameron's mother for whom she was always preparing some little surprise, a dainty gift, some fruit or flowers, a book that she thought might comfort and while away her loneliness, a restful ride at the early evening, all the little things that a thoughtful daughter might do for a mother. And Cameron's mother wrote him long letters about it all which would have delighted his heart during those dreary days if they could only have reached him then.

Ruth's letters to Cameron were full of the things she was doing, full of her sweet wise thoughts that seemed to be growing wiser every day. She had taken pictures of her Italian friends and introduced him to them one by one. She had filled every page with little word pictures of her daily life. It seemed a pity that he could not have had them just when he needed them most. It would have filled her with dismay if she could have known the long wandering journey that was before those letters before they would finally reach him; she might have been discouraged from writing them.

Little Mrs. Beck was suddenly sent for one Sunday

morning to attend her sister who was very ill, and she hastily called Ruth over the telephone and begged her to take her place at the Sunday school. Ruth promised to secure some one to teach the lesson, but found to her dismay that no one was willing to go at such short notice. And so, with trembling heart she knelt for a hasty petition that God would guide her and show her how to lead these simple people in the worship of the day.

As she stood before them trying to make plain in the broken, mixed Italian and English, the story of the blind man, which was the lesson for the day, there came over her a sense of her great responsibility. She knew that these people trusted her and that what she told them they would believe, and her heart lifted itself in a sharp cry for help, for light, to give to them. She felt an appalling lack of knowledge and experience herself. Where had she been all these young years of her life, and what had she been doing that she had not learned the way of life so that she might put it before them?

Before her sat a woman bowed with years, her face seamed with sorrow and hard work, and grimed with lack of care, a woman whose husband frequently beat her for attending Sunday school. There were four men on the back seat, hard workers, listening with eager eyes, assenting vigorously when she spoke of the sorrow on the earth. They, too, had seen trouble. They sat there patient, sad-eyed, wistful; what could she show them out of the Book of God to bring a light of joy to their faces? There were little children whose future looked so full of hard knocks and toil that it seemed a wonder they were willing to grow up knowing what was before them. The money that had smoothed her way thus far through life was not for them. The comfortable home and food and raiment and light and luxury that had made her life so full of ease were almost unknown to them. Had she anything better to offer them than mere earthly comforts which probably could never be theirs, no matter how hard they might strive? But, after all, money and ease could in no way soothe the pain of the heart, and she had come close enough already to these people to know they had each one his own heart's pain and sorrow to bear. There was one man who had lost five little children by death. That death had come in consequence of dirt and ignorance made it no easier to bear. The dirt and ignorance had not all been his fault. People who were wiser and had not cared to help were to blame. What was the remedy for the world's sorrow, the world's need?

Ruth knew in a general way that Jesus Christ was the Saviour of the world, that His name should be the remedy for evil; but how to put it to them in simple form, ah! that was it. It was Cameron's search for God, and it seemed that all the world was on the same search. But now to-day she had suddenly come on some of the footprints of the Man of Sorrow as He toiled over the mountains of earth searching for lost humanity, and her own heart echoed His love and sorrow for the world. She cried out in her helplessness for something to give to these wistful people.

Somehow the prayer must have been answered, for the little congregation hung upon her words, and one old man with deep creases in his forehead and kindly wrinkles around his eyes spoke out in meeting and said:

"I like God. I like Him good. I like Him all e time wi' mee! All e time. Ev'e where! Him live in my house!"

The tears sprang to her eyes with answering sympathy. Here in her little mission she had found a brother soul, seeking after God. She had another swift vision then of what the kinship of the whole world meant, and how Christ could love everybody.

After Sunday school was out little Sanda came stealing up to her:

"Mine brudder die," she said sorrowfully.

"What? Tony? The pretty fat baby? Oh, I'm so sorry!" said Ruth putting her arm tenderly around the little girl. "Where is your mother? I must go and see her."

Down the winding unkept road they walked, the delicately reared girl and the little Italian drudge, to the hovel where the family were housed, a tumbled-down affair of ancient stone, tawdrily washed over in some season past with scaling pink whitewash. The noisy abode of the family pig was in front of the house in the midst of a trim little garden of cabbage, lettuce, garlic, and tomatoes. But the dirty swarming little house usually so full of noise and good cheer was tidy to-day, and no guests hovered on the brief front stoop sipping from a friendly bottle, or playing the accordion. There was not an accordion heard in the community, for there had been a funeral that morning and every one was trying to be quiet out of respect for the bereaved parents.

And there in the open doorway, in his shirt sleeves, crouched low upon the step, sat the head of the house, his swarthy face bowed upon his knees, a picture of utter despair, and just beyond the mother's head was bowed upon her folded arms on the window seat, and thus they mourned in public silence before their little world.

Ruth's heart went out to the two poor ignorant creatures in their grief as she remembered the little dark child with the brown curls and glorious eyes who had resembled one of Raphael's cherubs, and thought how empty the mother's arms would be without him.

"Oh, Sanda, tell your mother how sorry I am!" she

said to the little girl, for the mother could not speak or understand English. "Tell her not to mourn so terribly, dear. Tell her that the dear baby is safe and happy with Jesus! Tell her she will go to Him some day."

And as the little girl interpreted her words, suddenly Ruth knew that what she was speaking was truth, truth she might have heard before but never recognized or realized till now.

The mother lifted her sorrowful face all tear-swollen and tried a pitiful smile, nodded to say she understood, then dropped sobbing again upon the window sill. The father lifted a sad face, not too sober, but blear-eyed and pitiful, too, in his hopelessness, and nodded as if he accepted the fact she had told but it gave him no comfort, and then went back to his own despair.

Ruth turned away with aching heart, praying: "Oh, God, they need you! Come and comfort them. I don't know how!" But somehow, on her homeward way she seemed to have met and been greeted by her Saviour.

It was so she received her baptism for the work that she was to do.

The next day permission came for her to go to France, and she entered upon her brief training.

"Don't you dread to have her go?" asked a neighbor of Aunt Rhoda.

"Oh, yes," sighed the good lady comfortably, "but then she is going in good company, and it isn't as if all the best people weren't doing it. Of course, it will be great experience for her, and I wouldn't want to keep her out of it. She'll meet a great many nice people over there that she might not have met if she had stayed at home. Everybody, they tell me, is at work over there. She'll be likely to meet the nobility. It isn't as if we didn't have friends there, too, who will be sure to invite her over week ends. If she gets tired she can go to them, you know. And really, I was glad to have something come up to take her away from that miserable little country slum she has been so crazy about. I was dreadfully afraid she would catch something there or else they would rob us and murder us and kidnap her some day."

And that was the way things presented themselves to Aunt Rhoda!

18

ALL day the shells had been flying thick and fast. When night settled down the fire was so continuous that one could trace the battle front by the reflection in the sky.

Cameron stood at his post under the stars and cried out in his soul for God. For days now Death had stalked them very close. His comrades had fallen all about him. There seemed to be no chance for safety. And where was God? Had He no part in all this Hell on earth? Did He not care? Would He not be found? All his seeking and praying and reading of the little book seemed to have brought God no nearer. He was going out pretty soon, in the natural order of the battle if things kept on, out into the other life, without having found the God who had promised that if he would believe, and if he would seek with all his heart he would surely find Him.

Once in a Y.M.C.A. hut on a Sunday night a great tenor came to entertain them, and sang almost the very words that the stranger back in the States had written in his little book:

"If with all your hearts ye truly seek Him ye shall ever surely find him. Thus saith your God!"

And ever since that song had rung its wonderful melody down deep in his heart he had been seeking, seeking in all the ways he knew, with a longing that would not be satisfied. And yet he seemed to have found nothing.

So now as he walked silently beneath the stars, looking up, his soul was crying out with the longing of despair to find a Saviour, the Christ of his soul. Amid all the shudderings of the battle-rent earth, the concussions of the bursting shells, could even God hear a soul's low cry?

Suddenly out in the darkness in front of him there flickered a tiny light, only a speck of a glint it was, the spark of a cigarette, but it was where it had no business to be, and it was Cameron's business to see that it was not there. They had been given strict orders that there must be no lights and no sounds to give away their position. Even though his thoughts were with the stars in his search for God, his senses were keen and on the alert. He sprang instantly and silently, appearing before the delinquent like a miracle.

"Halt!" he said under his breath. "Can that cigarette!"

"I guess you don't know who I am!" swaggered a voice thick and unnatural that yet had a familiar sound.

"It makes no difference who you are, you can't smoke on this post while I'm on duty. Those are my orders!" and with a quick motion he caught the cigarette from the loose lips and extinguished it, grinding it into the ground with his heel.

"I'll—have you—c-c-co-marshalled fer this!" stuttered the angry officer, stepping back unsteadily and raising his fist.

In disgust Cameron turned his back and walked away.

How had Wainwright managed to bring liquor with him to the front? Something powerful and condensed, no doubt, to steady his nerves in battle. Wainwright had ever been noted for his cowardice. His breath was heavy with it. How could a man want to meet death in such a way? He turned to look again, and Wainwright was walking unsteadily away across the line where they had been forbidden to go, out into the open where the shells were flying. Cameron watched him for an instant with mingled feelings. To think he called himself a man, and dared to boast of marrying such a woman as Ruth Macdonald. Well, what if he did go into danger and get killed! The world was better off without him! Cameron's heart was burning hot within him. His enemy was at last within his power. No one but himself had seen Wainwright move off in that direction where was certain death within a few minutes. It was no part of his duty to stop him. He was not supposed to know he had been drinking.

The whistle of a shell went ricocheting through the air and Cameron dropped as he had been taught to do, but lifted his eyes in time to see Wainwright throw up his arms, drop on the edge of the hill, and disappear. The shell plowed its way in a furrow a few feet away and Cameron rose to his feet. Sharply, distinctly, in a brief lull of the din about him he heard his name called. It sounded from down the hill, a cry of distress, but it did not sound like Wainwright's voice:

"Cameron! Come! Help!"

He obeyed instantly, although, strange to say, he had no thought of its being Wainwright. He crept cautiously out to the edge of the hill and looked over. The blare of the heavens made objects below quite visible. He could see Wainwright huddled as he had fallen. While he looked the injured man lifted his head, struggled to crawl feebly, but fell back again. He felt a sense of relief that at last his enemy was where he could do no more harm. Then, through the dim darkness he saw a figure coming toward the prostrate form, and stooping over to touch him. It showed white against the darkness and it paid no heed to the shell that suddenly whistled overhead. It half lifted the head of the fallen officer, and then straightened up and looked toward Cameron; and again, although there was no sound audible now in the din that the battle was making, he felt himself called.

A strange thrill of awe possessed him. Was that the Christ out there whom he had been seeking? And what did he expect of him? To come out there to his enemy? To the man who had been in many ways the curse of his young life?

Suddenly as he still hesitated a verse from his Testament which had often come to his notice returned clearly to his mind:

"If thou bringest thy gift to the altar, and there rememberest that thy brother hath aught against thee, leave there thy gift before the altar. First be reconciled to thy brother, and then come and offer thy gift."

Was this, then, what was required of him? Had his hate toward Wainwright been what had hindered him from finding God?

There was no time now to argue that this man was not his brother. The man would be killed certainly if he lay there many minutes. The opportunity would pass as quickly as it had come. The Christ he sought was out there expecting him to come, and he must lose no time in going to Him. How gladly would he have faced death to go to Him! But Wainwright! That was different! Could it be this that was required of him? Then back in his soul there echoed the words: "If with all your heart ye truly seek." Slowly he crept forward over the brow of the hill, and into the light, going toward that white figure above the huddled dark one; creeping painfully, with bullets ripping up the earth about him. He was going to the Christ, with all his heart—yes, all his heart! Even if it meant putting by his enmity forever!

Somewhere on the way he understood.

When he reached the fallen man there was no white figure there, but he was not surprised nor disappointed. The Christ was not there because he had entered into his heart. He had found Him at last!

Back at the base hospital they told Wainwright one day how Cameron had crawled with him on his back, out from under the searchlights amid the shells, and into safety. It was the only thing that saved his life, for if he had lain long with the wound he had got, there would have been no chance for him. Wainwright, when he heard it, lay thoughtful for a long time, a puzzled, half-sullen look on his face. He saw that everybody considered Cameron a hero. There was no getting away from that the rest of his life. One could not in decency be an enemy of a man who had saved one's life. Cameron had won out in a final round. It would not be good policy not to recognize it. It would be entirely too unpopular. He must make friends with him. It would be better to patronize him than to be patronized by him. Perhaps also, down in the depths of his fat selfish heart there was a little bit of gratitude mixed with it all. For he *did* love life, and he *was* a mortal coward.

So he sent for Cameron one day, and Cameron came. He did not want to come. He dreaded the interview worse than anything he had ever had to face before. But he came. He came with the same spirit he had gone out into the shell-fire after Wainwright. Because he felt that the Christ asked it of him.

He stood stern and grave at the foot of the little hospital cot and listened while Wainwright pompously thanked him, and told him graciously that now that he had saved his life he was going to put aside all the old quarrels and be his friend. Cameron smiled sadly. There was no bitterness in his smile. Perhaps just the least fringe of amusement, but no hardness. He even took the bandaged hand that was offered as a token that peace had come between them who had so long been at war. All the time were ringing in his heart the words: "With all your heart! With all your heart!" He had the Christ, what else mattered?

Somehow Wainwright felt that he had not quite made the impression on this strong man that he had hoped, and in an impulse to be more than gracious he reached his good hand under his pillow and brought forth an envelope.

When Corporal Cameron saw the writing on the envelope he went white under the tan of the battlefield, but he stood still and showed no other sign:

"When I get back home I'm going to be married," said the complacent voice, "and my wife and I will want you to come and take dinner with us some day. I guess you know who the girl is. She lives in Bryne Haven up on the hill. Her name is Ruth Macdonald. I've just had a letter from her. I'll have to write her how you saved my life. She'll want to thank you, too."

How could Cameron possibly know that that envelope addressed in Ruth Macdonald's precious handwriting contained nothing but the briefest word of thanks for an elaborate souvenir that Wainwright had sent her from France?

"What's the matter with Cammie?" his comrades asked one another when he came back to his company. "He looks as though he had lost his last friend. Did he care so much for that Wainwright guy that he saved? I'm sure I don't see what he sees in him. I wouldn't have taken the trouble to go out after him, would you?"

Cameron's influence had been felt quietly among his company. In his presence the men refrained from certain styles of conversation, when he sat apart and read his Testament they hushed their boisterous talk, and lately some had come to read with him. He was generally conceded to be the bravest man in their company, and when a fellow had to die suddenly he liked Cameron to hold him in his arms.

So far Cameron had not had a scratch, and the men had come to think he had a charmed life. More than he knew he was beloved of them all. More than they knew their respect for him was deepening into a kind of awe. They felt he had a power with him that they understood not. He was still the silent corporal. He talked not at all of his new-found experience, yet it shone in his face in a mysterious light. Even after he came from Wainwright with that stricken look, there was above it all a glory behind his eyes that not even that could change. For three days he went into the thick of the battle, moving from one hairbreadth escape to another with the calmness of an angel who knows his life is not of earth, and on the fourth day there came the awful battle, the struggle for a position that had been held by the enemy for four years, and that had been declared impregnable from the side of the Allies.

The boys all fought bravely and many fell, but foremost of them all passing unscathed from height to height, Corporal Cameron on the lead in fearlessness and spirit; and when the tide at last was turned and they stood triumphant among the dead, and saw the enemy retiring in disorder, it was Cameron who was still in the forefront, his white face and tattered uniform catching the last rays of the setting sun.

Later when the survivors had all come together one came to the captain with a white face and anxious eyes:

"Captain, where's Cammie? We can't find him anywhere."

"He came a half hour ago and volunteered to slip through the enemy's lines to-night and send us back a message," he said in husky tones. "But, captain, he was wounded!"

"He was?" The captain looked up startled. "He said nothing about it!"

"He wouldn't, of course," said the soldier. "He's that way. But he was wounded in the arm. I helped him bind it up."

"How bad?"

"I don't know. He wouldn't let me look. He said he would attend to it when he got back."

"Well, he's taken a wireless in his pocket and crept across No Man's Land to find out what the enemy is going to do. He's wearing a dead Jerry's uniform—!"

The captain turned and brushed the back of his hand across his eyes and a low sound between a sob and a whispered cheer went up from the gathered remnant as they rendered homage to their comrade.

For three days the messages came floating in, telling vital secrets that were of vast strategic value. Then the messages ceased, and the anxious officers and comrades looked in vain for word. Two more days passed—three—and still no sign that showed that he was alive, and the word went forth "Missing!" and "Missing" he was proclaimed in the newspapers at home.

That night there was a lull in the sector where Cameron's company was located. No one could guess what was going on across the wide dark space called No Man's Land. The captain sent anxious messages to other officers, and the men at the listening posts had no clue to give. It was raining and a chill bias sleet that cut like knives was driving from the northeast. Water trickled into the dugouts, and sopped through the trenches, and the men shuddered their way along dark passages and waited. Only scattered artillery fire lit up the heavens here and there. It was a night when all hell seemed let loose to have its way with earth. The watch paced back and forth and prayed or cursed, and counted the minutes till his watch would be up. Across the blackness of No Man's Land pock-marked with great shell craters, there raged a tempest, and even a Hun would turn his back and look the other way in such a storm.

Slowly, oh so slow that not even the earth would know it was moving, there crept a dark creature forth from the enemy line. A thing all of spirit could not have gone more invisibly. Lying like a stone as motionless for spaces uncountable, stirring every muscle with a controlled movement that could stop at any breath, lying under the very nose of the guard without being seen for long minutes, and gone when next he passed that way; slowly, painfully gaining ground, with a track of blood where the stones were cruel, and a holding of breath when the fitful flare lights lit up the way; covered at times by mud from nearby bursting shells; faint and sick, but continuing to creep; chilled and sore and stiff, blinded and bleeding and torn, shell holes and stones, and miring mud, slippery and sharp and never ending, the long, long trail—!

"Halt!" came a sharp, clear voice through the night.

"Pat! Come here! What is that?" whispered the guard. "Now watch! I'm sure I saw it move— There! I'm going to it!"

"Better look out!" But he was off and back with something in his arms. Something in a ragged blood-soaked German uniform.

They turned a shaded flash light into the face and looked:

"Pat, it's Cammie!" The guard was sobbing.

At sound of the dear old name the inert mass roused to action.

"Tell Cap—they're planning to slip away at five in the morning. Tell him if he wants to catch them he must do it *now!* Don't mind me! Go quick!"

The voice died away and the head dropped back.

With a last wistful look Pat was off to the captain, but the guard gathered Cameron up in his arms tenderly and nursed him like a baby, crooning over him in the sleet and dark, till Pat came back with a stretcher and some men who bore him to the dressing station lying inert between them.

While men worked over his silent form his message was flashing to headquarters and back over the lines to all the posts along that front. The time had come for the big drive. In a short time a great company of dark forms stole forth across No Man's Land till they seemed like a wide dark sea creeping on to engulf the enemy.

Next morning the newspapers of the world set forth in monstrous type the glorious victory and how the Americans had stolen upon the enemy and cut them off from the rest of their army, wiping out a whole salient.

But while the world was rejoicing, John Cameron lay on his little hard stretcher in the tent and barely breathed. He had not opened his eyes nor spoken again.

19

A nurse stepped up to the doctor's desk:

"A new girl is here ready for duty. Is there any special place you want her put?" she asked in a low tone.

The doctor looked up with a frown:

"One of those half-trained Americans, I suppose?" he growled. "Well, every little helps. I'd give a good deal for half a dozen fully trained nurses just now. Suppose you send her to relieve Miss Jennings. She can't do any harm to number twenty-nine."

"Isn't there any hope for him?" the nurse asked, a shade of sadness in her eyes.

"I'm afraid not!" said the doctor shortly. "He won't take any interest in living, that's the trouble. He isn't dying of his wounds. Something is troubling him. But it's no use trying to find out what. He shuts up like a clam."

The new nurse flushed outside the door as she heard herself discussed and shut her firm little lips in a determined way as she followed the head nurse down the long rows of cots to an alcove at the end where a screen shut the patient from view.

Miss Jennings, a plain girl with tired eyes, gave a few directions and she was left with her patient. She turned toward the cot and stopped with a soft gasp of recognition, her face growing white and set as she took in the dear familiar outline of the fine young face before her. Every word she had heard outside the doctor's office rang distinctly in her ears. He was dying. He did not want to live. With another gasp that was like a sob she slipped to her knees beside the cot, forgetful of her duties, of the ward outside, or the possible return of the nurses, forgetful of everything but that he was there, her hero of the years!

She reached for one of his hands, the one that was not bandaged, and she laid her soft cheek against it, and held her breath to listen. Perhaps even now behind that quiet face the spirit had departed beyond her grasp.

There was no flutter of the eyelids even. She could not see that he still breathed, although his hand was not cold, and his face when she touched it still seemed human. She drew closer in an agony of fear, and laid her lips against his cheek, and then her face softly, with one hand about his other cheek. Her lips were close to his ear now.

"John!" she whispered softly, "John! My dear knight!"

There was a quiver of the eyelids now, a faint hesitating sigh. She touched her lips to his and spoke his name again. A faint smile flickered over his features as if he were seeing other worlds of beauty that had no connection here. But still she continued to press her face against his cheek and whisper his name.

At last he opened his eyes, with a bewildered, wondering gaze and saw her. The old dear smile broke forth:

"Ruth! You here? Is this—heaven?"

"Not yet," she whispered softly. "But it's earth, and the war is over! I've come to help you get well and take you home! It's really you and you're not 'Missing' any more."

Then without any excuse at all she laid her lips on his forehead and kissed him. She had read her permit in his eyes.

His well arm stole out and pressed her to him hungrily:

"It's—really you and you don't belong to anybody else?" he asked, anxiously searching her face for his answer.

"Oh, John! I never did belong to anybody else but you. All my life ever since I was a little girl I've thought you were wonderful! Didn't you know that? Didn't you see down at camp? I'm sure it was written all over my face."

His hand crept up and pressed her face close against his.

"Oh, my darling!" he breathed, *"my* darling! The most wonderful girl in the world!"

When the doctor and nurse pushed back the screen and entered the little alcove the new nurse sat demurely at the foot of the cot, but a little while later the voice of the patient rang out joyously:

"Doctor, how soon can I get out of this? I think I've stayed here about long enough."

The wondering doctor touched his patient's forehead, looked at him keenly, felt his pulse with practised finger, and replied:

"I've been thinking you'd get to this spot pretty soon. Some beef tea, nurse, and make it good and strong. We've got to get this fellow on his feet pretty quick for I can see he's about done lying in bed."

Then the wounds came in for attention, and Ruth stood bravely and watched, quivering in her heart over the sight, yet never flinching in her outward calm.

When the dressing of the wounds was over the doctor stood back and surveyed his patient:

"Well, you're in pretty good shape now, and if you keep on you can leave here in about a week. Thank fortune there isn't any more front to go back to! But now, if you don't mind I'd like to know what's made this marvellous change in you?"

The light broke out on Cameron's face anew. He looked at the doctor smiling, and then he looked at Ruth, and reached out his hand to get hers:

"You see," he said, "I—we—Miss Macdonald's from my home town and—"

"I see," said the doctor looking quizzically from one happy face to the other, "but hasn't she always been from your home town?"

Cameron twinkled with his old Irish grin:

"Always," he said solemnly, "but, you see, she hasn't always been here."

"I see," said the doctor again looking quizzically into the sweet face of the girl, and doing reverence to her pure beauty with his gaze. "I congratulate you, corporal," he said, and then turning to Ruth he said earnestly: "And you, too, Madame. He is a man if there ever was one."

In the quiet evening when the wards were put to sleep and Ruth sat beside his cot with her hand softly in his, Cameron opened his eyes from the nap he was supposed to be taking and looked at her with his bright smile.

"I haven't told you the news," he said softly. "I have found God. I found Him out on the battlefield and He is great! It's all true! But you have to search for Him with *all* your heart, and not let any little old hate or anything else hinder you, or it doesn't do any good."

Ruth, with her eyes shining, touched her lips softly to

the back of his bandaged hand that lay near her and whispered softly:

"I have found Him, too, dear. And I realize that He has been close beside me all the time, only my heart was so full of myself that I never saw Him before. But, oh, hasn't He been wonderful to us, and won't we have a beautiful time living for Him together the rest of our lives?"

Then the bandaged hand went out and folded her close, and Cameron uttered his assent in words too sacred for other ears to hear.

About the Author

Grace Livingston Hill is well known as one of the most prolific writers of romantic fiction. Her personal life was fraught with joys and sorrows not unlike those experienced by many of her fictional heroines.

Born in Wellsville, New York, Grace nearly died during the first hours of life. But her loving parents and friends turned to God in prayer. She survived miraculously, thus her thankful father named her Grace.

Grace was always close to her father, a Presbyterian minister, and her mother, a published writer. It was from them that she learned the art of storytelling. When Grace was twelve, a close aunt surprised her with a hardbound, illustrated copy of one of Grace's stories. This was the beginning of Grace's journey into being a published author.

In 1892 Grace married Fred Hill, a young minister, and they soon had two lovely young daughters. Then came 1901, a difficult year for Grace—the year when, within months of each other, both her father and husband died. Suddenly Grace had to find a new place to live (her home was owned by the church where her husband had been pastor). It was a struggle for Grace to raise her young daughters alone, but through everything she kept writing. In 1902 she produced *The Angel of His Presence, The Story of a Whim,* and *An Unwilling Guest.* In 1903 her two books *According to the Pattern* and *Because of Stephen* were published.

It wasn't long before Grace was a well-known author, but she wanted to go beyond just entertaining her readers. She soon included the message of God's salvation through Jesus Christ in each of her books. For Grace, the most important thing she did was not write books but share the message of salvation, a message she felt God wanted her to share through the abilities he had given her.

In all, Grace Livingston Hill wrote more than one hundred books, all of which have sold thousands of copies and have touched the lives of readers around the world with their message of "enduring love" and the true way to lasting happiness: a relationship with God through his Son, Jesus Christ.

In an interview shortly before her death, Grace's devotion to her Lord still shone clear. She commented that whatever she had accomplished had been God's doing. She was only his servant, one who had tried to follow his teaching in all her thoughts and writing.

Don't miss these Grace Livingston Hill romance novels!

VOL.	TITLE	ORDER NUM.
1	Where Two Ways Met	07-8203-8-HILC
2	Bright Arrows	07-0380-4-HILC
3	A Girl to Come Home To	07-1017-7-HILC
4	Amorelle	07-0310-3-HILC
5	Kerry	07-2044-X-HILC
6	All through the Night	07-0018-X-HILC
7	The Best Man	07-0371-5-HILC
8	Ariel Custer	07-1686-8-HILC
9	The Girl of the Woods	07-1016-9-HILC
10	Crimson Roses	07-0481-9-HILC
11	More Than Conqueror	07-4559-0-HILC
12	Head of the House	07-1309-5-HILC
14	Stranger within the Gates	07-6441-2-HILC
15	Marigold	07-4037-8-HILC
16	Rainbow Cottage	07-5731-9-HILC
17	Maris	07-4042-4-HILC
18	Brentwood	07-0364-2-HILC
19	Daphne Deane	07-0529-7-HILC
20	The Substitute Guest	07-6447-1-HILC
21	The War Romance of the Salvation Army	07-7911-8-HILC
22	Rose Galbraith	07-5726-2-HILC
23	Time of the Singing of Birds	07-7209-1-HILC
24	By Way of the Silverthorns	07-0341-3-HILC
25	Sunrise	07-5941-9-HILC
26	The Seventh Hour	07-5884-6-HILC
27	April Gold	07-0011-2-HILC
28	White Orchids	07-8150-3-HILC
29	Homing	07-1494-6-HILC
30	Matched Pearls	07-3895-0-HILC
32	Coming through the Rye	07-0357-X-HILC
33	Happiness Hill	07-1487-3-HILC
34	The Patch of Blue	07-4809-3-HILC
36	Patricia	07-4814-X-HILC
37	Silver Wings	07-5914-1-HILC
38	Spice Box	07-5939-7-HILC
39	The Search	07-5831-5-HILC
40	The Tryst	07-7340-3-HILC
41	Blue Ruin	07-0349-9-HILC

VOL.	TITLE	ORDER NUM.
42	A New Name	07-4718-6-HILC
43	Dawn of the Morning	07-0530-0-HILC
44	The Beloved Stranger	07-0303-0-HILC
60	Miranda	07-4298-2-HILC
61	Mystery Flowers	07-4613-9-HILC
63	The Man of the Desert	07-3955-8-HILC
64	Miss Lavinia's Call	07-4360-1-HILC
77	The Ransom	07-5143-4-HILC
78	Found Treasure	07-0911-X-HILC
79	The Big Blue Soldier	07-0374-X-HILC
80	The Challengers	07-0362-6-HILC
81	Duskin	07-0574-2-HILC
82	The White Flower	07-8149-X-HILC
83	Marcia Schuyler	07-4036-X-HILC
84	Cloudy Jewel	07-0474-6-HILC
85	Crimson Mountain	07-0472-X-HILC
86	The Mystery of Mary	07-4632-5-HILC
87	Out of the Storm	07-4778-X-HILC
88	Phoebe Deane	07-5033-0-HILC
89	Re-Creations	07-5334-8-HILC
90	Sound of the Trumpet	07-6107-3-HILC
91	A Voice in the Wilderness	07-7908-8-HILC
92	The Honeymoon House	07-1393-1-HILC
93	Katharine's Yesterday	07-2038-5-HILC

If you are unable to find any of these titles at your local bookstore, you may call Tyndale's toll-free number **1-800-323-9400, X-214** for ordering information. Or you may write for pricing to **Tyndale Family Products, P.O. Box 448, Wheaton, IL 60189-0448.**